D0759714

P9-BXU-812

*Hunted and Harried*

A LEAP FOR LIFE—Page 88

# Hunted and Harried

## A Tale of the Scottish Covenanters

*by*

## R.M. BALLANTYNE

*Author of*
*The Coral Island, Blue Lights,*
*Martin Rattler, etc., etc.*

THE VISION FORUM, INC.
SAN ANTONIO, TEXAS

*Reprinted from the 1892 Classic by R.M. Ballantyne*

Sixth Printing
*Revised Edition*

Copyright © 2008–2010 The Vision Forum, Inc.
All Rights Reserved.

*"Where there is no vision, the people perish."*

www.visionforum.com

ISBN-10  1-934554-03-0
ISBN-13  978-1-934554-03-6

The cloth covers in this series are color-coded to represent the geographic region of each story. The regions and their respective colors are as follows:

| | |
|---|---|
| NORTH AMERICA—*Forest Green* | SOUTH AMERICA—*Wheat* |
| SOUTH PACIFIC—*Light Blue* | ARCTIC REGIONS—*Grey* |
| EUROPE—*Navy Blue* | AFRICA—*Sienna* |
| ASIA—*Red* | |

PRINTED IN THE UNITED STATES OF AMERICA

 The "Scotch Thistle," the floral emblem of Scotland, serves as the emblem of the R.M. Ballantyne Series published by Vision Forum.

# CONTENTS

## CHAPTER IX

## CHAPTER X

## CHAPTER XI

## CHAPTER XII

# Chapter I

ON THE HUNT.

On a brilliant summer morning in the last quarter of the seventeenth century a small troop of horsemen crossed the ford of the river Cairn, in Dumfriesshire, not far from the spot where stands the little church of Irongray, and, gaining the road on the western bank of the stream, wended their way towards the moors and uplands which lie in the neighbourhood of Skeoch Hill.

The dragoons, for such they were, trotted rapidly along the road that led into the solitudes of the hills, with all the careless dash of men whose interests are centered chiefly on the excitements of the passing hour, yet with the unflagging perseverance of those who have a fixed purpose in view - their somewhat worn aspect and the mud with which they were bespattered, from jack-boot to iron headpiece, telling of a long ride over rugged ground.

The officer in command of the party rode a little in advance. Close behind him followed two troopers, one of whom was a burly middle-aged man with a stern, swarthy countenance; the other a youth whose tall frame was scarcely, if at all, less powerful than that of his comrade-in-arms, though much more elegant in form, while his youthful and ruddy, yet masculine, countenance suggested that he must at that time have been but a novice in the art of war.

This youth alone, of all the party, had a somewhat careworn and sad expression on his brow. It could hardly have been the result of fatigue, for there was more of ease and vigour in his carriage than in that of any of his companions.

"We should be near the river by this time, Glendinning," said the leader of the party, reining in and addressing the swarthy trooper.

"Ay, sir, the Cluden rins jist ayont the turn o' the

road there," replied the man. "Ye'll hear the roar o' the fa' in a meenit or twa."

Even as he spoke the dull growl of a cataract was heard, and, a few minutes later, the party came upon the ford of the river.

It was situated not many yards below the picturesque waterfall, which is now spanned by the Routen Bridge, but which, at that time, was unbridged—at all events, if a bridge had previously existed, it had fallen in or been carried away—and the wild gorge was impassable.

The sound of the fall alone told of its vicinity, for a dense mass of foliage hid it completely from the troopers' view until they had surmounted the steep bank on the other side of the stream.

"Are you well acquainted with this man Black?" asked the leader of the party as they emerged from the thick belt of trees and shrubs by which the Cluden was shaded, and continued their journey on the more open ground beyond.

"I ken him weel, sir," answered the trooper. "Andrew Black was an auld freend o' mine, an' a big, stoot, angry man he is—kindly disposed, nae doot, when ye let him alane, but a perfe't deevil incarnate when he's roosed. He did me an ill turn ance that I've no paid him off for *yet*."

"I suppose, then," said the officer, "that your guiding us so willingly to his cottage is in part payment of this unsettled debt?"

"Maybe it is," replied the trooper grimly.

"They say," continued the other, "that there is some mystery about the man; that somehow nobody can catch him. Like an eel he has slipped through our fellows' fingers and disappeared more than once, when they thought they had him quite safe. It is said that on one occasion he managed even to give the slip to Claverhouse himself, which, you know, is not easy."

"That may be, sir, but he'll no slip through my fingers gin I ance git a grup o' his thrapple," said the swarthy man, with a revengeful look.

"We must get a grip of him somehow," returned the officer, "for it is said that he is a sly helper of the rebels—though it is as difficult to convict as to catch him; and as this gathering, of which our spies have brought information, is to be in the neighbourhood of his house, he is sure to be mixed up with it."

"Nae doot o' that, sir, an' so we may manage to kill

twa birds wi' ae stane. But I'm in a diffeeculty noo, sir, for ye ken I'm no acquaint wi' this country nae farer than the Cluden ford, an' here we hae come to a fork i' the road."

The party halted as he spoke, while the perplexed guide stroked his rather long nose and looked seriously at the two roads, or bridle-paths, into which their road had resolved itself, and each of which led into very divergent parts of the heathclad hills.

This guide, Glendinning, had become acquainted with Black at a time when the latter resided in Lanarkshire, and, as he had just said, was unacquainted with the region through which they now travelled beyond the river Cluden. After a short conference the officer in command decided to divide the party and explore both paths.

"You will take one man, Glendinning, and proceed along the path to the right," he said; "I will try the left. If you discover anything like a house or cot within a mile or two you will at once send your comrade back to let me know, while you take up your quarters in the cottage and await my coming. Choose whom you will for your companion."

"I choose Will Wallace, then," said Glendinning, with a nod to the young trooper whom we have already introduced.

The youth did not seem at all flattered by the selection, but of course obeyed orders with military promptitude, and followed his comrade for some time in silence, though with a clouded brow.

"It seems to me," said the swarthy trooper, as they drew rein and proceeded up a steep ascent at a walk, "that ye're no' sae pleased as ye might be wi' the wark we hae on hand."

"Pleased!" exclaimed the youth, whose tone and speech seemed to indicate him an Englishman, "how can I be pleased when all I have been called on to do since I enlisted has been to aid and abet in robbery, cruelty, and murder? I honour loyalty and detest rebellion as much as any man in the troop, but if I had known what I now know I would never have joined you."

Glendinning gazed at his companion in amazement. Having been absent on detached service when Will Wallace had joined—about three weeks previously—he was ignorant both as to his character and his recent experiences. He had chosen him on the present occasion simply on account of his youth and magnificent physique.

"I doot I've made a mistake in choosin' *you*," said Glendinning with some asperity, after a few moments, "but it's ower late noo to rectifee't. What ails ye, lad? What hae ye seen?"

"I have seen what I did not believe possible," answered the other with suppressed feeling. "I have seen a little boy tortured with the thumbscrews, pricked with bayonets, and otherwise inhumanly treated because he would not, or could not, tell where his father was. I have seen a man hung up to a beam by his thumbs because he would not give up money which perhaps he did not possess. I have seen a woman tortured by having lighted matches put between her fingers because she would not, or could not, tell where a conventicle was being held. I did not, indeed, see the last deed actually done, else would I have cut down the coward who did it. The poor thing had fainted and the torture was over when I came upon them. Only two days ago I was ordered out with a party who pillaged the house of a farmer because he refused to take an oath of allegiance, which seems to have been purposely so worded as to make those who take it virtually bondslaves to the King, and which makes him master of the lives, properties, and consciences of his subjects—and all this done in the King's name and by the King's troops!"

"An' what pairt did *you* tak' in these doin's?" asked Glendinning with some curiosity.

"I did my best to restrain my comrades, and when they were burning the hayricks, throwing the meal on the dunghill, and wrecking the property of the farmer, I cut the cords with which they had bound the poor fellow to his chair and let him go free."

"Did onybody see you do that?"

"I believe not; though I should not have cared if they had. I'm thoroughly disgusted with the service. I know little or nothing of the principles of these rebels—these fanatics, as you call them—but tyranny or injustice I cannot stand, whether practised by a king or a beggar, and I am resolved to have nothing more to do with such fiendish work."

"Young man," said the swarthy comrade in a voice of considerable solemnity, "ye hae obviously mista'en your callin'. If you werena new to thae pairts, ye would ken that the things ye objec' to are quite common. Punishin' an' harryin' the rebels and fanatics— *Covenanters*, they ca' theirsels—has been gaun on for years ower a' the land. In my opeenion it's weel deserved, an' naething that ye can do or say wull prevent it, though what ye do an' say is no' unlikely to cut short yer ain career by means o' a rope roond yer thrapple. But losh! man, I wonder ye haena heard about thae matters afore now."

"My having spent the last few years of my life in an out-of-the-way part of Ireland may account for that," said Wallace. "My father's recent death obliged my mother to give up her farm and return to her native town of Lanark, where she now lives with a brother. Poverty and the urgency of a cousin have induced me, unfortunately, to take service with the dragoons."

"After what ye've said, hoo am I to coont on yer helpin' me e'noo?" asked Glendinning.

"As long as I wear the King's uniform you may count on my obeying orders unless I am commanded to break the plainest laws of God," answered the young man. "As our present business is only to discover the cottage of Andrew Black, there seems likely to be no difficulty between us just now."

"H'm! I'm no' sure o' that; but if ye'll tak' my advice, lad, ye'll haud yer tongue aboot thae matters. If Clavers heard the half o' what ye've said to me, he'd send ye into the next warl' withoot gieing ye time to say yer prayers. Freedom of speech is no permitted at the present time in Scotland—unless it be the right kind of speech, and—"

He stopped, for at that moment two young girls suddenly appeared at a bend of the road in front of them. They gazed for a moment at the soldiers in evident surprise, and then turned as if to fly, but Glendinning put spurs to his horse and was beside them in a moment. Leaping to the ground, he seized the girls roughly by their arms as they clung together in alarm. One of the two was a dark-eyed little child. The other was fair, unusually pretty, and apparently about fifteen or sixteen years of age.

The trooper proceeded to question them sharply.

"Be gentle," said Will Wallace sternly, as he rode up, and, also dismounting, stood beside them. "No fear of their running away now."

The swarthy trooper pretended not to hear, but nevertheless relaxed his grip and merely rested his hand upon the fair girl's shoulder as he said to the other—

"Now, my wee doo, ye canna be far frae hame, I's be sworn. What's yer name?"

"Aggie Wilson," answered the child at once.

"And yours?"

"Jean Black," replied the blonde timidly.

"Oho! an' yer faither's name is Andrew, an' his hoose is close by, I'll be bound, so ye'll be guid eneuch to show us the way till't. But first, my bonny lass, ye'll gie me a—"

Slipping his arm round the waist of the terrified blonde, the trooper rudely attempted to terminate his sentence in a practical manner; but before his lips could touch her face he received a blow from his comrade that sent him staggering against a neighbouring tree.

Blazing with astonishment and wrath, Glendinning drew his sword and sprang at his companion, who, already full of indignation at the memory of what he had been so recently compelled to witness, could ill brook the indignity thus offered to the defenceless girl. His weapon flashed from its sheath on the instant, and for a few moments the two men cut and thrust at each other with savage ferocity. Wallace, however, was too young and unused to mortal strife to contemplate with indifference the possibility of shedding the blood of a comrade. Quickly recovering himself, he stood entirely on the defensive, which his vigorous activity enabled him easily to do. Burning under the insult he had received, Glendinning felt no such compunctions. He pushed his adversary fiercely, and made a lunge at last which not only passed the sword through the left sleeve of the youth's coat, but slightly wounded his arm. Roused to uncontrollable anger by this, Will Wallace fetched his opponent a blow so powerful that it beat down his guard, rang like a hammer on his iron headpiece, and fairly hurled the man into the ditch at the roadside.

Somewhat alarmed at this sudden result, the youth hastily pulled him out, and, kneeling beside him, anxiously examined his head. Much to his relief he found that there was no wound at all, and that the man was only stunned. After the examination, Wallace observed that the girls had taken advantage of the fray to make their escape.

Indignation and anger having by that time evaporated, and his judgment having become cool, Wallace began gradually to appreciate his true position, and to feel exceedingly uncomfortable. He had recklessly expressed opinions and confessed to actions which would of themselves ensure his being disgraced and cast into prison, if not worse; he had almost killed one of his own comrades, and had helped two girls to escape who could probably have assisted in the accomplishment of the duty on which they had been despatched. His case, he suddenly perceived, was hopeless, and he felt that he was a lost man.

Will Wallace was quick of thought and prompt in action. Carefully disposing the limbs of his fallen comrade, and resting his head comfortably on a grassy bank, he cast a hurried glance around him.

On his left hand and behind him lay the rich belt of woodland that marked the courses of the rivers Cluden and Cairn. In front stretched the moors and hills of the ancient district of Galloway, at that time given over to the tender mercies of Graham of Claverhouse. Beside him stood the two patient troop-horses, gazing quietly at the prostrate man, as if in mild surprise at his unusual stillness.

Beyond this he could not see with the physical eye; but with the mental orb he saw a dark vista of ruined character, blighted hopes, and dismal prospects. The vision sufficed to fix his decision. Quietly, like a warrior's wraith, he sheathed his sword and betook himself to the covert of the peat-morass and the heather hill.

He was not the first good man and true who had sought the same shelter.

At the time of which we write Scotland had for many years been in a woeful plight—with tyranny draining her life-blood, cupidity grasping her wealth, hypocrisy and bigotry misconstruing her motives and falsifying her character. Charles II filled the throne. Unprincipled men, alike in Church and State, made use of their position and power to gain their own ends and enslave the people. The King, determined to root out Presbytery from Scotland, as less subservient to his despotic aims, and forcibly to impose Prelacy on her as a stepping-stone to Popery, had no difficulty in finding ecclesiastical and courtly bravos to carry out his designs; and for a long series of dismal years persecution stalked red-handed through the land.

Happily for the well-being of future generations, our covenanting forefathers stood their ground with Christian heroism, for both civil and religious liberty were involved in the struggle. Their so-called fanaticism consisted in a refusal to give up the worship of God after the manner dictated by conscience and practised by their forefathers; in declining to attend the ministry of the ignorant, and too often vicious, curates forced upon them; and in refusing to take the oath of allegiance just referred to by Will Wallace.

Conventicles, as they were called—or the gathering together of Christians in houses and barns, or on the hillsides, to worship God—were illegally pronounced illegal by the King and Council; and disobedience to the tyrannous law was punished with imprisonment, torture, confiscation of property, and death. To enforce these penalties the greater part of Scotland—especially the south and west—was overrun by troops, and treated as if it were a conquered country. The people—holding that in some matters it is incumbent to "obey God rather than man," and that they were bound "not to forsake the assembling of themselves together"—resolved to set the intolerable law at defiance, and went armed to the hill-meetings.

They took up arms at first, however, chiefly, if not solely, to protect themselves from a licentious soldiery, who went about devastating the land, not scrupling to rob and insult helpless women and children, and to shed innocent blood. Our Scottish forefathers, believing—in common with the lower animals and lowest savages—that it was a duty to defend their females and little ones, naturally availed themselves of the best means of doing so.

About this time a meeting, or conventicle, of considerable importance was appointed to be held among the secluded hills in the neighbourhood of Irongray; and Andrew Black, the farmer, was chosen to select the particular spot, and make the preliminary arrangements.

Now this man Black is not easily described, for his was a curiously compound character. To a heart saturated with the milk of human kindness was united a will more inflexible, if possible, than that of a Mexican mule; a frame of Herculean mould, and a spirit in which profound gravity and reverence waged incessant warfare with a keen appreciation of the ludicrous. Peacefully inclined in disposition, with a tendency to believe well of all men, and somewhat free and easy in the formation of his opinions, he was very unwilling to resist authority; but the love of truth and justice was stronger within him than the love of peace.

In company with his shepherd, Quentin Dick—a man of nearly his own size and build—Andrew Black proceeded to a secluded hollow in Skeoch Hill to gather and place in order the masses of rock which were to form the seats of the communicants at the contemplated religious gathering—which seats remain to this day in the position they occupied at that time, and are familiarly known in the district as "the Communion stones of Irongray."

# Chapter II

The night was dark and threatening when Andrew Black and his shepherd left their cottage, and quickly but quietly made for the neighbouring hill. The weather was well suited for deeds of secrecy, for gusts of wind, with an occasional spattering of rain, swept along the hill-face, and driving clouds obscured the moon, which was then in its first quarter.

At first the two men were obliged to walk with care, for the light was barely sufficient to enable them to distinguish the sheep-track which they followed, and the few words they found it necessary to speak were uttered in subdued tones. Jean Black and her cousin

Aggie Wilson had reported their *rencontre* with the two dragoons, and Quentin Dick had himself seen the main body of the troops from behind a heather bush on his way back to the farm, therefore caution was advisable. But as they climbed Skeoch Hill, and the moon shed a few feeble rays on their path, they began to converse more freely. For a few minutes their intercourse related chiefly to sheep and the work of the farm, for both Andrew and his man were of that sedate, imperturbable nature which is not easily thrown off its balance by excitement or danger. Then their thoughts turned to the business in hand.

"Nae fear o' the sodgers comin' here on a nicht like this," remarked Andrew, as a squall nearly swept the blue bonnet off his head.

"Maybe no," growled Quentin Dick sternly, "but I've heard frae Tam Chanter that servants o' that Papist Earl o' Nithsdale, an' o' the scoondrel Sir Robert Dalziel, hae been seen pokin' their noses aboot at Irongray. If they git wund o' the place, we're no likely to hae a quiet time o't. Did ye say that the sodgers ill-used the bairns?"

"Na!—ane o' them was inclined to be impident,

but the ither, a guid-lookin' young felly, accordin' to Jean, took their pairt an' quarrelled wi' his comrade, sae that they cam to loggerheeds at last, but what was the upshot naebody kens, for the bairns took to their heels an' left them fechtin'."

"An' what if they sud fin' yer hoose an' the bairns unproteckit?" asked the shepherd.

"They're no likely to fin' the hoose in a nicht like this, man; an' if they do, they'll fin' naebody but Ramblin' Peter there, for I gied the lassies an' the women strick orders to tak' to the hidy-hole at the first soond o' horses' feet."

By this time the men had reached a secluded hollow in the hill, so completely enclosed as to be screened from observation on all sides. They halted here a few moments, for two dark forms were seen in the uncertain light to be moving about just in front of them.

"It's them," whispered Andrew.

"Whae?" asked the shepherd.

"Alexander McCubine an' Edward Gordon."

"Guid an' safe men baith," responded Quentin; "ye better gie them a cry."

Andrew did so by imitating the cry of a plover. It was replied to at once.

"The stanes are big, ye see," explained Andrew, while the two men were approaching. "It'll tak' the strength o' the fowr o' us to lift some o' them."

"We've got the cairn aboot finished," said McCubine as he came up. He spoke in a low voice, for although there was no probability of any one being near, they were so accustomed to expect danger because of the innumerable enemies who swarmed about the country, that caution had almost become a second nature.

Without further converse the four men set to work in silence. They completed a circular heap, or cairn, of stones three or four feet high, and levelled the top thereof to serve as a table or a pulpit at the approaching assembly. In front of this, and stretching towards a sloping brae, they arranged four rows of very large stones to serve as seats for the communicants, with a few larger stones between them, as if for the support of rude tables of plank. It took several hours to complete the work. When it was done Andrew Black surveyed it with complacency, and gave it as his opinion that it was a "braw kirk, capable o' accommodatin' a

congregation o' some thoosands, mair or less." Then
the two men, Gordon and McCubine, bidding him and
the shepherd good-night, went away into the darkness
from which they had emerged.

"Whar'll they be sleepin' the nicht?" asked the
shepherd, as he and Andrew turned homeward.

"I' the peat-bog, I doot, for I daurna tak' them hame
whan the dragoons is likely to gie us a ca'; besides, the
hidy-hole wull be ower fu' soon. Noo, lad," he added,
as they surmounted a hillock, from which they had a
dim view of the surrounding country, "gang ye doon
an' see if ye can fin' oot onything mair aboot thae
sodgers. I'll awa' hame an see that a's right there."

They parted, the shepherd turning sharp off to the
right, while the farmer descended towards his cottage.
He had not advanced above half the distance when
an object a little to the left of his path induced him to
stop. It resembled a round stone, and was too small to
have attracted the attention of any eye save one which
was familiar with every bush and stone on the ground.
Grasping a stout thorn stick which he carried, Andrew
advanced towards the object in question with catlike
caution until quite close to it, when he discovered that

it was the head of a man who was sleeping soundly under a whin-bush. A closer inspection showed that the man wore an iron headpiece, a soldier's coat, and huge jack-boots.

"A dragoon and a spy!" thought Andrew, while he raised his cudgel, the only weapon he carried, and frowned. But Andrew was a merciful man; he could not bring himself to strike a sleeping man, even though waking him might entail a doubtful conflict, for he could see that the trooper's hand grasped the hilt of his naked sword. For a few moments he surveyed the sleeper, as if calculating his chances, then he quietly dropped his plaid, took off his coat, and untying his neckcloth, laid it carefully on one side over a bush. Having made these preparations, he knelt beside Will Wallace—for it was he—and grasped him firmly by the throat with both hands.

As might have been expected, the young trooper attempted to spring up, and tried to use his weapon; but, finding this to be impossible at such close quarters, he dropped it, and grappled the farmer with all his might; but Andrew, holding on to him like a vice, placed his knee upon his chest and held him firmly down.

"It's o' nae manner o' use to strive, ye see," said Andrew, relaxing his grip a little; "I've gotten ye, an' if ye like to do my biddin' I'll no be hard on ye."

"If you will let me rise and stand before me in fair fight, I'll do your business if not your bidding," returned Wallace in a tone of what may be termed stern sulkiness.

"Div ye think it's likely I'll staund before you in fair fecht, as you ca'd—you wi' a swurd, and me wi' a bit stick, my lad? Na, na, ye'll hae to submit, little though ye like it."

"Give me the stick, then, and take you the sword, I shall be content," said the indignant trooper, making another violent but unsuccessful effort to free himself.

"It's a fair offer," said Andrew, when he had subdued the poor youth a second time, "an' reflec's favourably on yer courage, but I'm a man o' peace, an' have no thirst for bloodshed—whilk is more than ye can say, young man; but if ye'll let me tie yer hands thegither, an' gang peaceably hame wi' me, I's promise that nae mischief'll befa' ye."

"No man shall ever tie my hands together as long as

there is life in my body," replied the youth.

"Stop, stop, callant!" exclaimed Andrew, as Will was about to renew the struggle. "The pride o' youth is awful. Hear what I've gotten to say to ye, man, or I'll hae to throttle ye ootright. It'll come to the same thing if ye'll alloo me to tie ane o' *my* hands to ane o' yours. Ye canna objec' to that, surely, for I'll be your prisoner as muckle as you'll be mine—and that'll be fair play, for we'll leave the swurd lyin' on the brae to keep the bit stick company."

"Well, I agree to that," said Wallace, in a tone that indicated surprise with a dash of amusement.

"An' ye promise no' to try to get away when you're tied to—when *I'm* tied to *you?*"

"I promise."

Hereupon the farmer, reaching out his hand, picked up the black silk neckcloth which he had laid aside, and with it firmly bound his own left wrist to the right wrist of his captive, talking in a grave, subdued tone as he did so.

"Nae doot the promise o' a spy is hardly to be lippened to, but if I find that ye're a dishonourable man, ye'll find that I'm an uncomfortable prisoner to be tied to. Noo, git up, lad, an' we'll gang hame thegither."

On rising, the first thing the trooper did was to turn and take a steady look at the man who had captured him in this singular manner.

"Weel, what d'ye think o' me?" asked Andrew, with what may be termed a grave smile.

"If you want to know my true opinion," returned Wallace, "I should say that I would not have thought, from the look of you, that you could have taken mean advantage of a sleeping foe."

"Ay—an' I would not have thought, from the look o' *you*," retorted Andrew, "that ye could hae sell't yersel' to gang skulkin' aboot the hills as a spy upon the puir craters that are only seekin' to worship their Maker in peace."

Without further remark Andrew Black, leaving his coat and plaid to keep company with the sword and stick, led his prisoner down the hill.

Andrew's cottage occupied a slight hollow on the hillside, which concealed it from every point of the compass save the high ground above it. Leading the trooper up to the door, he tapped gently, and was

ANDREW BLACK'S PRISONER—Page 37

promptly admitted by some one whom Wallace could not discern, as the interior was dark.

"Oh, Uncle Andrew! I'm glad ye've come, for Peter hasna come back yet, an' I'm feared somethin' has come ower him."

"Strike a light, lassie. I've gotten haud o' a spy here, an' canna weel do't mysel'."

When a light was procured and held up, it revealed the pretty face of Jean Black, which underwent a wondrous change when she beheld the face of the prisoner.

"Uncle Andrew!" she exclaimed, "this is nae spy. He's the man that cam' to the help o' Aggie an' me against the dragoon."

"Is that sae?" said Black, turning a look of surprise on his prisoner.

"It is true, indeed, that I had the good fortune to protect Jean and her friend from an insolent comrade," answered Wallace; "and it is also true that that act has been partly the cause of my deserting to the hills, being starved for a day and a night, and taken prisoner now as a spy."

"Sir," said Andrew, hastily untying the kerchief that

bound them together, "I humbly ask your pardon. Moreover, it's my opeenion that if ye hadna been starvin' ye wadna have been here 'e noo, for ye're uncommon teuch. Rin, lassie, an' fetch some breed an' cheese. Whar's Marion an' Is'b'l?"

"They went out to seek for Peter," said Jean, as she hastened to obey her uncle's mandate.

At that moment a loud knocking was heard at the door, and the voice of Marion, one of the maid-servants, was heard outside. On the door being opened, she and her companion Isabel burst in with excited looks and the information, pantingly given, that the "sodgers were comin'."

"Haud yer noise, lassie, an' licht the fire—pit on the parritch pat. Come, Peter, let's hear a' aboot it."

Ramblin' Peter, who had been thus named because of his inveterate tendency to range over the neighbouring hills, was a quiet, undersized, said-to-be weak-minded boy of sixteen years, though he looked little more than fourteen. No excitement whatever ruffled his placid countenance as he gave his report—to the effect that a party of dragoons had been seen by him not half an hour before, searching evidently for his master's cottage.

"They'll soon find it," said the farmer, turning quickly to his domestics— "Away wi' ye, lassies, and hide."

The two servant-girls, with Jean and her cousin Aggie Wilson, ran at once into an inner room and shut the door. Ramblin' Peter sat stolidly down beside the fire and calmly stirred the porridge-pot, which was nearly full of the substantial Scottish fare.

"Noo, sir," said Black, turning to Will Wallace, who had stood quietly watching the various actors in the scene just described, "yer comrades'll be here in a wee while. May I ask what ye expect?"

"I expect to be imprisoned at the least, more probably shot."

"Hm! pleasant expectations for a young man, nae doot. I'm sorry that it's oot o' my power to stop an' see the fun, for the sodgers have strange suspicions aboot me, so I'm forced to mak' mysel' scarce an' leave Ramblin' Peter to do the hospitalities o' the hoose. But before I gang awa' I wad fain repay ye for the guid turn ye did to my bairns. If ye are willin' to shut yer eyes an' do what I tell ye, I'll put you in a place o' safety."

"Thank you, Mr. Black," returned Wallace; "of course I shall only be too glad to escape from the consequences of my unfortunate position; but do not misunderstand me: although neither a spy nor a Covenantor I am a loyal subject, and would not now be a deserter if that character had not been forced upon me, first by the brutality of the soldiers with whom I was banded, and then by the insolence of my comrade-in-arms to your daughter—"

"Niece; niece," interrupted Black; "I wish she *was* my dauchter, bless her bonny face! Niver fear, sir, I've nae doot o' yer loyalty, though you an' yer freends misdoot mine. I claim to be as loyal as the best o' ye, but there's nae dictionary in *this* warld that defines loyalty to be slavish submission o' body an' sowl to a tyrant that fears naether God nor man. The quastion noo is, Div ye want to escape and wull ye trust me?"

The sound of horses galloping in the distance tended to quicken the young trooper's decision. He submitted to be blindfolded by his captor.

"Noo, Peter," said Andrew, as he was about to lead Wallace away, "ye ken what to dae. Gie them plenty to eat; show them the rum bottle, let them hae the rin o' the hoose, an' say that I bade ye treat them weel."

"Ay," was Ramblin' Peter's laconic reply.

Leading his captive out at the door, round the house, and re-entering by a back door, apparently with no other end in view than to bewilder him, Andrew went into a dark room, opened some sort of door—to enter which the trooper had to stoop low—and conducted him down a steep, narrow staircase.

The horsemen meanwhile had found the cottage and were heard at that moment tramping about in front, and thundering on the door for admittance.

Wallace fancied that the door which closed behind him must be of amazing thickness, for it shut out almost completely the sounds referred to.

On reaching the foot of the staircase, and having the napkin removed from his eyes, he found himself in a long, low, vaulted chamber. There was no one in it save his guide and a venerable man who sat beside a deal table, reading a document by the light of a tallow candle stuck in the mouth of a black bottle.

The soldiers, meanwhile, having been admitted by Ramblin' Peter, proceeded to question that worthy as to Andrew Black and his household. Not being satisfied of the truth of his replies they proceeded to apply torture in order to extract confession. It was the first time that this mode of obtaining information had been used in Black's cottage, and it failed entirely, for Ramblin' Peter was staunch, and, although inhumanly thrashed and probed with sword-points, the poor lad remained dumb, insomuch that the soldiers at length set him down as an idiot, for he did not even cry out in his agonies—excepting in a curious, half-stifled manner—because he knew well that if his master were made aware by his cries of what was going on he would be sure to hasten to the rescue at the risk of his life.

Having devoured the porridge, drunk the rum, and destroyed a considerable amount of the farmer's produce, the lawless troopers, who seemed to be hurried in their proceedings at that time, finally left the place.

About the time that these events were taking place in and around Black's cottage, bands of armed men with women and even children were hastening towards the same locality to attend the great "conventicle," for which the preparations already described were being made.

The immediate occasion of the meeting was the desire of the parishioners of the Reverend John Welsh, a great-grandson of John Knox, to make public avowal, at the Communion Table, of their fidelity to Christ and their attachment to the minister who had been expelled from the church of Irongray; but strong sympathy induced many others to attend, not only from all parts of Galloway and Nithsdale, but from the distant Clyde, the shores of the Forth, and elsewhere; so that the roads were crowded with people making for the rendezvous—some on foot, others on horseback. Many of the latter were gentlemen of means and position, who, as well as their retainers, were more or less well armed and mounted. The Reverend John Blackadder, the "auld" minister of Troqueer—a noted hero of the Covenant, who afterwards died a prisoner on the Bass Rock—travelled with his party all the way from Edinburgh, and a company of eighty horse proceeded to the meeting from Clydesdale.

Preliminary services, conducted by Mr. Blackadder and Mr. Welsh, were held near Dumfries on the Saturday, but at these the place of meeting on the Sabbath was only vaguely announced as "a hillside in Irongray," so anxious were they to escape being disturbed by their enemies, and the secret was kept so well that when the Sabbath arrived a congregation of above three thousand had assembled round the Communion stones in the hollow of Skeoch Hill.

Sentinels were posted on all the surrounding heights. One of these sentinels was the farmer Andrew Black, with a cavalry sword belted to his waist, and a rusty musket on his shoulder. Beside him stood a tall stalwart youth in shepherd's costume.

"Yer ain mother wadna ken ye," remarked Andrew with a twinkle in his eyes.

"I doubt that," replied the youth; "a mother's eyes are keen. I should not like to encounter even Glendinning in my present guise."

As he spoke the rich melody of the opening psalm burst from the great congregation and rolled in softened cadence towards the sentinels.

# Chapter III

THE TRUE AND THE FALSE AT WORK.

The face of nature did not seem propitious to the great gathering on Skeoch Hill. Inky clouds rolled athwart the leaden sky, threatening a deluge of rain, and fitful gusts of wind seemed to indicate the approach of a tempest. Nevertheless the elements were held in check by the God of nature, so that the solemn services of the day were conducted to a close without discomfort, though not altogether without interruption.

Several of the most eminent ministers, who had been expelled from their charges, were present on this occasion. Besides John Welsh of Irongray, there were Arnot of Tongland, Blackadder of Troqueer, and Dickson of Rutherglen—godly men who had for many years suffered persecution and imprisonment, and were ready to lay down their lives in defence of religious liberty. The price set upon the head of that "notour traitor, Mr. John Welsh," dead or alive, was 9000 merks. Mr. Arnot was valued at 3000!

These preached and assisted at different parts of the services, while the vast multitude sat on the sloping hillside, and the mounted men drew up on the outskirts of the congregation, so as to be within sound of the preachers' voices, and, at the same time, be ready for action on the defensive if enemies should appear.

Andrew Black and his companion stood for some time listening, with bowed heads, to the slow sweet music that floated towards them. They were too far distant to hear the words of prayer that followed, yet they continued to stand in reverent silence for some time, listening to the sound—Black with his eyes closed, his young companion gazing wistfully at the distant landscape, which, from the elevated position on which they stood, lay like a magnificent panorama spread out before them. On the left the level lands

bordering the rivers Cairn and Nith stretched away
to the Solway, with the Cumberland mountains in the
extreme distance; in front and on the right lay the
wild, romantic hill-country of which, in after years, it
was so beautifully written:—

> "O bonnie hills of Galloway oft have I stood to see,
> At sunset hour, your shadows fall, all darkening on
>        the lea;
> While visions of the buried years came o'er me in
>        their might—
> As phantoms of the sepulchre—instinct with
>        inward light!
> The years, the years when Scotland groaned
>        beneath her tyrant's hand!
> And 'twas not for the heather she was called 'the
>        purple land.'
> And 'twas not for her loveliness her children
>        blessed their God—
> *But for secret places of the hills, and the mountain*
>        *heights untrod.*"

"Who was the old man I found in what you call your
hidy-hole?" asked Wallace, turning suddenly to his
companion.

"I'm no' sure that I have a right to answer that," said

Black, regarding Will with a half-serious, half-amused look. "Hooever, noo that ye've ta'en service wi' me, and ken about my hidy-hole, I suppose I may trust ye wi' a' my secrets."

"I would not press you to reveal any secrets, Mr. Black, yet I think you are safe to trust me, seeing that you know enough about my own secrets to bring me to the gallows if so disposed."

"Ay, I hae ye there, lad! But I'll trust ye on better grunds than that. I believe ye to be an honest man, and that's enough for me. Weel, ye maun ken, it's saxteen year since I howkit the hidy-hole below my hoose, an' wad ye believe it?—they've no fund it oot yet! Not even had a suspeecion o't, though the sodgers hae been sair puzzled, mony a time, aboot hoo I managed to gie them the slip. An' mony's the puir body, baith gentle and simple, that I've gien food an' shelter to whae was very likely to hae perished o' cauld an' hunger, but for the hidy-hole. Among ithers I've often had the persecuited ministers doon there, readin' their Bibles or sleepin' as comfortable as ye like when the dragoons was drinkin', roarin', an' singin' like deevils ower their heids. My certies! if Clavers, or Sherp, or Lauderdale

had an inklin' o' the hunderd pairt o' the law-brekin'
that I've done, it's a gallows in the Gressmarkit as high
as Haman's wad be ereckit for me, an' my heed an'
hauns, may be, would be bleachin' on the Nether Bow.
Humph! but they've no' gotten me yet!"

"And I sincerely hope they never will," remarked
Wallace; "but you have not yet told me the name of
the old man."

"I was comin' to him," continued Black; "but
wheniver I wander to the doin's o' that black-hearted
Cooncil, I'm like to lose the threed o' my discoorse.
Yon is a great man i' the Kirk o' Scotland. They ca'
him Donald Cargill. The adventures that puir man has
had in the coorse o' mair nor quarter o' a century wad
mak' a grand story-buik. He has no fear o' man, an'
he's an awfu' stickler for justice. I'se warrant he gied
ye some strang condemnations o' the poors that be."

"Indeed he did not," said Wallace. "Surely you
misjudge his character. His converse with me was
entirely religious, and his chief anxiety seemed to be to
impress on me the love of God in sending Jesus Christ
to redeem a wicked world from sin. I tried to turn the
conversation on the state of the times, but he gently

turned it round again to the importance of being at peace with God, and giving heed to the condition of my own soul. He became at last so personal that I did not quite like it. Yet he was so earnest and kind that I could not take offence."

"Ay, ay," said Black in a musing tone, "I see. He clearly thinks that yer he'rt needs mair instruction than yer heed. Hm! maybe he's right. Hooever, he's a wonderfu' man; gangs aboot the country preachin' everywhere altho' he kens that the sodgers are aye on the look-oot for him, an' that if they catch him it's certain death. He wad have been at this communion nae doot, if he hadna engaged to preach somewhere near Sanquhar this vera day."

"Then he has left the hidy-hole by this time, I suppose?"

"Ye may be sure o' that, for when there is work to be done for the Master, Donal' Cargill doesna let the gress grow under his feet."

"I'm sorry that I shall not see him again," returned the ex-trooper in a tone of regret, "for I like him much."

Now, while this conversation was going on, a

portion of the troop of dragoons which had been out in search of Andrew Black was sent under Glendinning (now a sergeant) in quest of an aged couple named Mitchell, who were reported to have entertained intercommuned, *IE* outlawed, persons; attended conventicles in the fields; ventured to have family worship in their cottages while a few neighbours were present, and to have otherwise broken the laws of the Secret Council.

This Council, which was ruled by two monsters in human form, namely, Archbishop Sharp of Saint Andrews and the Duke of Lauderdale, having obtained full powers from King Charles the Second to put down conventicles and enforce the laws against the fanatics with the utmost possible rigour, had proceeded to carry out their mission by inviting a host of half, if not quite, savage Highlanders to assist them in quelling the people. This host, numbering, with 2000 regulars and militia, about 10,000 men, eagerly accepted the invitation, and was let loose on the south and western districts of Scotland about the beginning of the year, and for some time ravaged and pillaged the land as if it had been an enemy's country. They were thanked by the King for so readily agreeing to assist in reducing the Covenanters to obedience to "Us and Our laws," and were told to take up free quarters among the disaffected, to disarm such persons as they should suspect, to carry with them instruments of torture wherewith to subdue the refractory, and in short to act very much in accordance with the promptings of their own desires. Evidently the mission suited these men admirably, for they treated all parties as disaffected, with great impartiality, and plundered, tortured, and insulted to such an extent that after about three months of unresisted depredation, the shame of the thing became so obvious that Government was compelled to send them home again. They had accomplished nothing in the way of bringing the Covenanters to reason; but they had desolated a fair region of Scotland, spilt much innocent blood, ruined many families, and returned to their native hills heavily laden with booty of every kind like a victorious army. It is said that the losses caused by them in the county of Ayr alone amounted to over 11,000 pounds sterling.

The failure of this horde did not in the least check the proceedings of Sharp or Lauderdale or their like-minded colleagues. They kept the regular troops and militia moving about the land, enforcing their idiotical and wicked laws at the point of the sword. We say idiotical advisedly, for what could give stronger evidence of mental incapacity than the attempt to enforce a bond upon all landed proprietors, obliging themselves and their wives, children, and servants, as well as all their tenants and cottars, with their wives, children, and servants, to abstain from conventicles, and not to receive, assist, or even speak to, any forfeited persons, intercommuned ministers, or vagrant preachers, but to use their utmost endeavours to apprehend all such? Those who took this bond were to receive an assurance that the troops should not be quartered on their lands—a matter of considerable importance—for this quartering involved great expense and much destruction of property in most cases, and absolute ruin in some.

After the battle of the Pentland Hills (in 1666), in which the Covenanters, driven to desperation, made an unsuccessful effort to throw off the tyrannical yoke, severer laws were enacted against them. Their wily persecutor, also being well aware of the evil

influence of disagreement among men, threw a bone
of contention among them in the shape of royal acts
of *Indulgence*, as they were styled, by which a certain
number of the ejected ministers were permitted to
preach on certain conditions, but only within their
own parishes. To preach at a separate meeting in a
private house subjected the minister to a fine of 5000
merks (about 278 pounds). To preach in the fields
was to incur the penalty of death and confiscation of
property. And these arbitrary laws were not merely
enacted for intimidation. They were rigorously
enforced. The curates in many cases became mere
spies and Government informers. Many of the best
men in the land laid down their lives rather than cease
to proclaim the Gospel of love and peace and goodwill
in Jesus Christ. Of course their enemies set them down
as self-willed and turbulent fanatics. It has ever been,
and ever will be, thus with men who are indifferent to
principle. They will not, as well as cannot, understand
those who are ready to fight, and, if need be, die for
truth! Their unspoken argument seems to be: "You
profess to preach peace, love, submission to authority,
etc.; very good, stand to your principles. Leave all sorts

of carnal fighting to us. Obey us. Conform humbly to our arrangements, whatever they are, and all will be well; but dare to show the slightest symptom of restiveness under what you style our injustice, tyranny, cruelty, etc., and we will teach you the submission which you preach but fail to practise by means of fire and sword and torture and death!"

Many good men and true, with gentle spirits, and it may be somewhat exalted ideas about the rights of Royalty, accepted the Indulgence as being better than nothing, or better than civil war. No doubt, also, there were a few—neither good men nor true—who accepted it because it afforded them a loophole of escape from persecution. Similarly, on the other side, there were good men and true, who, with bolder hearts, perhaps, and clearer brains, it may be, refused the Indulgence as a presumptuous enactment, which cut at the roots of both civil and religious liberty, as implying a right to withhold while it professed to give, and which, if acquiesced in, would indicate a degree of abject slavery to man and unfaithfulness to God that might sink Scotland into a condition little better than that of some eastern nations at the present day. Thus was the camp of the Covenanters divided. There were also more subtle divisions, which it is not necessary to mention here, and in both camps, of course there was an infusion, especially amongst the young men, of that powerful element—love of excitement and danger for their own sake, with little if any regard to principle, which goes far in all ages to neutralise the efforts and hamper the energies of the wise.

Besides the acts of Indulgence, another and most tyrannical measure, already mentioned, had been introduced to crush if possible the Presbyterians. *Letters of intercommuning* were issued against a great number of the most distinguished Presbyterians, including several ladies of note, by which they were proscribed as rebels and cut off from all society. A price, amounting in some instances to 500 pounbds sterling, was fixed on their heads, and every person, not excepting their nearest of kin, was prohibited from conversing with or writing to them, or of aiding with food, clothes, or any other necessary of life, on pain of being found guilty of the same crimes as the intercommuned persons.

The natural result of such inhuman laws was that men and women in hundreds had to flee from their homes and seek refuge among the dens and caves of the mountains, where many were caught, carried off to prison, tried, tortured, and executed; while of those who escaped their foes, numbers perished from cold and hunger, and disease brought on by lying in damp caves and clefts of the rocks without food or fire in all weathers. The fines which were exacted for so-called offences tempted the avarice of the persecutors and tended to keep the torch of persecution aflame. For example, Sir George Maxwell of Newark was fined a sum amounting to nearly 8000 pounds sterling for absence from his Parish Church, attendance at conventicles, and disorderly baptisms—IE for preferring his own minister to the curate in the baptizing of his children! Hundreds of somewhat similar instances might be given. Up to the time of which we write (1678) no fewer than 17,000 persons had suffered for attending field meetings, either by fine, imprisonment, or death.

Such was the state of matters when the party of dragoons under command of Sergeant Glendinning rode towards the Mitchells' cottage, which was not far from Black's farm. The body of soldiers being too small to venture to interrupt the communion on Skeoch Hill, Glendinning had been told to wait in the neighbourhood and gather information while his officer, Captain Houston, went off in search of reinforcements.

"There's the auld sinner himsel'," cried the Sergeant as the party came in sight of an old, whitehaired man seated on a knoll by the side of the road. "Hallo! Jock Mitchell, is that you? Come doon here directly, I want to speak t'ye."

The old man, being stone deaf, and having his back to the road, was not aware of the presence of the dragoons, and of course took no notice of the summons.

"D'ye hear!" shouted the Sergeant savagely, for he was ignorant of the old man's condition.

Still Mitchell did not move. Glendinning, whose disposition seemed to have been rendered more brutal since his encounter with Wallace, drew a pistol from his holster and presented it at Mitchell.

"Answer me," he shouted again, "or ye're a deed man."

Mitchell did not move... There was a loud report, and next moment the poor old man fell dead upon the ground.

It chanced that Ramblin' Peter heard the report, though he did not witness the terrible result, for he was returning home from the Mitchells' cottage at the time, after escorting Jean Black and Aggie Wilson thither. The two girls, having been forbidden to attend the gathering on Skeoch Hill, had resolved to visit the Mitchells and spend the Sabbath with them. Peter had accompanied them and spent the greater part of the day with them, but, feeling the responsibility of his position as the representative of Andrew Black during his absence, had at last started for home.

A glance over a rising ground sufficed to make the boy turn sharp round and take to his heels. He was remarkably swift of foot. A few minutes brought him to the cottage door, which he burst open.

"The sodgers is comin', grannie!" (He so styled the old woman, though she was no relation.)

"Did ye see my auld man?"

"No."

"Away wi' ye, bairns," said Mrs. Mitchell quickly but quietly. "Oot by the back door an' doon the burnside; they'll niver see ye for the busses."

"But, grannie, we canna leave you here alone,"

remonstrated Jean with an anxious look.

"An' I can fecht!" remarked Peter in a low voice, that betrayed neither fear nor excitement.

"The sodgers can do nae harm to *me*," returned the old woman firmly. "Do my bidding, bairns. Be aff, I say!"

There was no resisting Mrs. Mitchell's word of command. Hastening out by the back door just as the troopers came in sight, Peter and his companions, diving into the shrubbery of the neighbouring streamlet, made their way to Black's farm by a circuitous route. There the girls took shelter in the house, locking the door and barring the windows, while Peter, diverging to the left, made for the hills like a hunted hare.

Andrew was standing alone at his post when the lithe runner came in sight. Will Wallace had left him by that time, and was listening entranced to the fervid exhortations of Dickson of Rutherglen.

"The sodgers!" gasped Peter, as he flung himself down to rest.

"Comin' this way, lad?"

"Na. They're at the Mitchells."

"A' safe at the ferm?" asked Andrew quickly.

"Ay, I saw the lasses into the hoose."

"Rin to the meetin' an' gie the alarm. Tell them to send Wallace an' Quentin here wi' sax stoot men—weel airmed—an' anither sentry, for I'm gaun awa'."

Almost before the sentence was finished Ramblin' Peter was up and away, and soon the alarming cry arose from the assembly, "The dragoons are upon us!"

Instantly the Clydesdale men mounted and formed to meet the expected onset. The men of Nithsdale were not slow to follow their example, and Gordon of Earlstoun, a tried and skilful soldier, put himself at the head of a large troop of Galloway horse. Four or five companies of foot, also well armed, got ready for action, and videttes and single horsemen were sent out to reconnoitre. Thus, in a moment, was this assembly of worshippers transformed into a band of Christian warriors, ready to fight and die for their families and liberties.

But the alarm, as it turned out, was a false one. Glendinning, informed by spies of the nature of the gathering, was much too sagacious a warrior to oppose his small force to such overwhelming odds. He contented himself for the present with smaller game.

After continuing in the posture of defence for a considerable time, the assembly dispersed, those who were defenceless being escorted by armed parties to the barns and cottages around. As they retired from the scene the windows of heaven were opened, and the rain, which had been restrained all day, came down in torrents, and sent the Cairn and Cluden red and roaring to the sea.

But long before this dispersion took place, Andrew Black, with Quentin Dick, Will Wallace, Ramblin' Peter, and six sturdy young men, armed with sword, gun, and pistol, had hurried down the hill to succour the Mitchells, if need be, and see to the welfare of those who had been left behind in the farm.

# Chapter IV

Being ignorant, as we have said, of the cruel murder of old Mitchell, Ramblin' Peter's report had not seriously alarmed Black. He concluded that the worst the troopers would do would be to rob the poor old couple of what money they found in their possession, oblige them to take the Oath of Supremacy, drink the health of King and bishops, and otherwise insult and plunder them. Knowing the Mitchells intimately, he had no fear that their opposition would invite severity. Being very fond of them, however, he resolved, at the risk of his life, to prevent as far as possible the threatened indignity and plunder.

"They're a douce auld pair," he remarked to Will Wallace as they strode down the hillside together, "quiet an' peaceable, wi' naething to speak o' in the way of opeenions—somethin' like mysel'—an' willin' to let-be for let-be. But since the country has been ower-run by thae Hielanders an' sodgers, they've had little peace, and the auld man has gie'n them a heap o' trouble, for he's as deaf as a post. Peter says the pairty o' dragoons is a sma' ane, so I expect the sight o' us'll scare them away an' prevent fechtin'."

"It may be so," said Wallace, "and of course I shall not fail you in this attempt to protect your old friends; but, to tell you the truth, I don't quite like this readiness on the part of you Covenanters to defy the laws, however bad they may be, and to attack the King's troops. The Bible, which you so often quote, inculcates longsuffering and patience."

"Hm! there speaks yer ignorance," returned the farmer with a dash of cynicism in his tone. "Hoo mony years, think ye, are folk to submit to tyranny an' wrang an' fierce oppression for nae sin whatever against the laws o' God or the land? Are twunty, thretty, or forty years no' enough to warrant oor claim to lang-sufferin'? Does submission to law-brekin' on the pairt o' Government, an' lang-continued, high-handed oppression frae King, courtier, an' prelate, accompanied wi' barefaced plunder and murder—does *that* no' justifiee oor claim to patience? To a' this the Covenanters hae submitted for mony weary years withoot rebellion, except maybe in the metter o' the Pentlands, when a wheen o' us were driven to desperation. But I understand your feelin's, lad, for I'm a man o' peace by natur', an' would gladly submit to injustice to keep things quiet—*if possable*; but some things are *no'* possable, an' the Bible itsel' says we're to live peaceably wi' a' men only 'as much as in us lies.'"

The ex-trooper was silent. Although ignorant of the full extent of maddening persecution to which not merely the Covenanters but the people of Scotland generally had been subjected, his own limited experience told him that there was much truth in what his companion said; still, like all loyal-hearted men, he shrank from the position of antagonism to Government.

"I agree with you," he said, after a few minutes' thought, "but I have been born, I suppose, with a profound respect for law and legally constituted authority."

"Div ye think, lad," returned Black, impressively, "that naebody's been born wi' a high respec' for law but yersel'? I suppose ye admit that the King is bound to respec' the law as weel as the people?"

"Of course I do. I am no advocate of despotism."

"Weel then," continued the farmer with energy, "in the year saxteen forty-ane, an' at ither times, kings an' parliaments hae stamped the Covenants o' Scotland as bein' pairt o' the law o' this land—whereby freedom o' conscience an' Presbyterian worship are secured to us a'. An' here comes Chairles the Second an' breks the law by sendin' that scoondrel the Duke o' Lauderdale here wi' full poors to dae what he likes— an' Middleton, a man wi' nae heart an' less conscience, that was raised up frae naething to be a noble, nae less! My word, nobles are easy made, but they're no' sae easy unmade! An' this Lauderdale maks a cooncil wi' Airchbishop Sherp—a traiter and a turncoat—an' a wheen mair like himsel', and they send sodgers oot ower the land to eat us up an' cram Prelacy doon oor throats, an' curates into oor poo'pits whether we wull or no'. An' that though Chairles himsel' signed the Covenant at the time he was crooned! Ca' ye *that* law or legally constituted authority?"

Although deeply excited by this brief recital of his country's wrongs, Black maintained the quiet expression of feature and tone of voice that were habitual to him. Further converse on the subject was interrupted by their arrival at the farm, where they found all right save that Jean and Aggie were in a state of tearful anxiety about their poor neighbours.

While the farmer was seeing to the security of his house and its arrangements, preparatory to continuing the march to the Mitchells' cottage, the rest of the party stood about the front door conversing. Will Wallace was contemplating Jean Black with no little admiration, as she moved about the house. There was something peculiarly attractive about Jean. A winsome air and native grace, with refinement of manner unusual in one of her station, would have stamped her with a powerful species of beauty even if she had not possessed in addition a modest look and fair young face.

The ex-trooper was questioning, in a dreamy way,

whether he had ever before seen such a pretty and agreeable specimen of girlhood, when he experienced a shock of surprise on observing that Jean had gone to a neighbouring spring for water and was making something very like a signal to him to follow her.

The surprise was mingled with an uncomfortable feeling of regret, for the action seemed inconsistent with the maiden's natural modesty.

"Forgie me, sir," she said, "for being so bold, but oh! sir, if ye knew how anxious I am about Uncle Black, ye would understand—he is wanted so much, an' there's them in the hidy-hole that would fare ill if he was taken to prison just now. If—ye—would—"

"Well, Jean," said Will, sympathising with the struggle it evidently cost the girl to speak to him—"don't hesitate to confide in me. What would you have me do?"

"Only to keep him back frae the sodgers if ye can. He's such an awfu' man to fecht when he's roosed, that he's sure to kill some o' them if he's no' killed himsel'. An' it'll be ruin to us a' an' to the Mitchells too, if—"

She was interrupted at this point by Black himself calling her name.

"Trust me," said Wallace earnestly, "I understand what you wish, and will do my best to prevent evil."

A grateful look was all the maiden's reply as she hurried away.

Our hero's perplexity as to how this promise was to be fulfilled was, however, needless, for on reaching the Mitchells' hut it was found that the troopers had already left the place; but the state of things they had left behind them was enough to stir deeply the pity and the indignation of the party.

Everything in confusion—broken furniture, meal and grain scattered on the floor, open chests and cupboards—told that the legalised brigands had done their worst. Poor Mrs. Mitchell had objected to nothing that they said or did or proposed to her. She feebly drank the health of King and prelates when bidden to do so, and swore whatever test-oaths they chose to apply to her till they required her to admit that the King was lord over the kirk and the conscience. Then her spirit fired, and with a firm voice she declared that no king but Christ should rule over her kirk or conscience—to which she boldly added that she *had* attended conventicles, and would do so again!

Having obtained all they wanted, the dragoons went away, leaving the old woman among the ruins of her home, for they probably did not consider it worth while carrying off a prisoner who would in all likelihood have died on the road to prison.

In the midst of all the noise and confusion it had struck the old woman as strange that they never once asked about her husband. After they had gone, however, the arrival of two neighbours bearing his dead body revealed the terrible reason. She uttered no cry when they laid his corpse on the floor, but sat gazing in horror as if turned to stone. Thus Black and his friends found her.

She could not be roused to speak, and looked, after a few minutes, like one who had not realised the truth.

In this state she was conveyed to Black's cottage and handed over to Jean, whom every one seemed intuitively to regard as her natural comforter. The poor child led her into her own room, sat down beside her on the bed, laid the aged head on her sympathetic bosom and sobbed as if her heart was breaking. But no response came from the old woman, save that once or twice she looked up feebly and said, "Jean, dear, what ails ye?"

In the Council Chamber at Edinburgh, Lauderdale, learning on one occasion that many persons both high and low had refused to take the bond already referred to, which might well have been styled the bond of slavery, bared his arm in fury, and, smiting the table with his fist, swore with a terrific oath that he would "force them to take the bond."

What we have described is a specimen of the manner in which the force was sometimes applied. The heartless despot and his clerical coadjutors had still to learn that tyranny has not yet forged the weapon that can separate man from his God.

"What think ye noo?" asked Andrew Black, turning to Wallace with a quiet but stern look, after old Mrs. Mitchell had been carried in, "what think ye *noo*, lad, o' us Covenanters an' oor lack o' lang-sufferin' an' oor defyin' the laws? Aren't these laws we *ought* to defy, but havena properly defied yet, laws illegally made by a perjured King and an upstart Cooncil?"

"Mr. Black," said the ex-trooper, seizing his companion's hand with an iron grip, "from this day forward I am with you—heart and soul."

Little did Wallace think, when he came to this decision, that he had still stronger reason for his course of action than he was aware of at the moment.

It was night when Mrs. Mitchell was brought into the farm-house, and preparations were being made for a hasty meal, when Ramblin' Peter came in with the news that a number of people in the Lanarkshire district had been intercommuned and driven from their homes— amongst others David Spence, Will Wallace's uncle, with whom his mother had taken up her abode.

The distracted looks of poor Wallace on hearing this showed the powerful effect the news had upon him.

"Keep yersel' quiet, noo," said Black in an encouraging tone, as he took the youth's arm and led him out of the house. "These are no' times to let our hearts rin awa wi' oor heids. Yer mither must be looked after; but i' the meantime let me tell ye that yer uncle Daavid is a douce, cliver felly, an' fears naething i' this warld. If he did, he wadna be amang the intercommuned. Be sure he's no' the man to leave his sister Maggie in trouble. Of course ye'll be wantin' to be aff to look after her."

"Of course—instantly," said Wallace.

"Na. Ye'll hae yer supper first—an' a guid ain—for ye'll need it. Have patience, noo, an' listen to me, for I'll do the very best I can for ye in this strait—an' it's no muckle ye can do for yersel' withoot help."

There was something so decided yet kindly and reassuring in the farmer's tone and manner that Wallace felt relieved in spite of his anxieties, and submitted to his guidance in all things. Black then explained that he had a friend in Lanark who owed him money on lambs sold to him the previous year; that he meant to send his man Quentin Dick first to collect that money, and then proceed to Edinburgh, for the purpose of making further arrangements there about cattle.

"Noo," continued Black, "I've gotten a mither as weel as you, an' she lives in the Can'lemaker Raw, close to the Greyfriars' Kirkyaird—where they signed the Covenants, ye ken. Weel, I wad advise you to gang to Lanark wi' Quentin, an' when ye find yer mither tak' her to Edinbro' an' let her live wi' my mither i' the meantime, till we see what the Lord has in store for this puir persecuted remnant. I'm sorry to pairt wi' ye, lad, sae unexpectedly, but in thae times, when folk are called on to pairt wi' their heids unexpectedly, we mauna compleen."

"I'll take your advice gladly," said Wallace. "When will Quentin Dick be ready to start?"

"In less than an hour. The moon'll be up soon after that. It's o' nae use startin' on sae dark a nicht till she's up, for ye'll hae to cross some nasty grund. Noo, lad, though I'm no a minister, my advice to ye is, to gang doon into the hidy-hole an' pray aboot this matter. Niver mind the folk ye find there. They're used to prayin'. It's my opeenion that if there was less preachin' an' mair prayin', we'd be a' the better for 't. It's a thrawn warld we live in, but we're bound to mak' the best o't."

Although not much in the habit of engaging in prayer—save at the formal periods of morning and evening—our ex-trooper was just then in the mood to take his friend's advice. He retired to the place of refuge under Black's house, where he found several people who had evidently been at the communion on Skeoch Hill. These were engaged in earnest conversation, and took little notice of him as he entered. The place was very dimly lighted. One end of the low vaulted chamber was involved in obscurity. Thither the youth went and knelt down. From infancy his mother had taught him "to say his prayers," and had sought to induce him to pray. It is probable that the first time he really did so was in that secret chamber where, in much anxiety of soul, he prayed for herself.

After a hasty but hearty supper, he and Quentin Dick set out on their night journey. They carried nothing with them except two wallets, filled, as Wallace could not help thinking, with a needlessly large amount of provisions. Of course they were unarmed, for they travelled in the capacity of peaceful drovers, with plaids on their shoulders, and the usual staves in their hands.

"One would think we were going to travel for a month in some wilderness, to judge from the weight of our haversacks," observed Wallace, after trudging along for some time in silence.

"Maybe we'll be langer than a month," returned Quentin, "ann the wulderness hereaway is warse than the wulderness that Moses led his folk through. They had manna there. Mony o' us hae *naething* here."

Quentin Dick spoke with cynicism in his tone, for he was a stern straightforward man, on whom injustice told with tremendous power, and who had not yet been taught by adversity to bow his head to man and restrain his indignation.

Before Wallace had time to make any rejoinder, something like the appearance of a group of horsemen in front arrested them. They were still so far distant as to render their tramp inaudible. Indeed they could not have been seen at all in so dark a night but for the fact that in passing over the crest of a hill they were for a moment or two dimly defined against the sky.

"Dragoons—fowr o' them," muttered Quentin. "We'll step aside here an' let them gang by."

Clambering up the somewhat rugged side of the road, the two men concealed themselves among the bushes, intending to wait till the troopers should pass.

"What can they be doing in this direction, I wonder?" whispered Wallace.

"My freend," answered Quentin, "dinna whisper when ye're hidin'. Of a' the sounds for attractin' attention an' revealin' secrets a whisper is the warst.

Speak low, if ye maun speak, but sometimes it's wiser no to speak ava'. Dootless the sodgers'll be giein' Andrew Black a ca', but he kens brawly hoo to tak' care o' himsel'."

When the horseman approached it was seen that they were driving before them a boy, or lad, on foot. Evidently they were compelling him to act as their guide.

"It's Ramblin' Peter they've gotten haud o', as sure as I'm a leevin' man," said the shepherd with a low chuckle; "I'd ken him amang a thoosand by the way he rins."

"Shall we not rescue him?" exclaimed Wallace, starting up.

"Wheesht! keep still, man. Nae fear o' Peter. He'll lead them in amang the bogs o' some peat-moss or ither, gie them the slip there, an' leave them to find their way oot."

Just as the troop trotted past an incident occurred which disconcerted the hiders not a little. A dog which the soldiers had with them scented them, stopped, and after snuffing about for a few seconds, began to bark furiously. The troop halted at once and challenged.

"Tak' nae notice," remarked Quentin in a low voice, which went no farther than his comrade's ear.

A bright flash and sharp report followed the challenge, and a ball whistled through the thicket.

"Ay, fire away," soliloquised Quentin. "Ye seldom hit when ye can see. It's no' likely ye'll dae muckle better i' the dark."

The dog, however, having discovered the track of the hidden men, rushed up the bank towards them. The shepherd picked up a stone, and, waiting till the animal was near enough, flung it with such a true aim that the dog went howling back to the road. On this a volley from the carbines of the troopers cut up the bushes all around them.

"That'll dae noo. Come awa', Wull," said the shepherd, rising and proceeding farther into the thicket by a scarce visible footpath. "The horses canna follow us here unless they hae the legs an' airms o' puggies. As for the men, they'd have to cut a track to let their big boots pass. We may tak' it easy, for they're uncommon slow at loadin'."

In a few minutes the two friends were beyond all danger. Returning then to the road about a mile farther on, they continued to journey until they had left the scene of the great communion far behind them, and when day dawned they retired to a dense thicket in a hollow by the banks of a little burn, and there rested till near sunset, when the journey was resumed. That night they experienced considerable delay owing to the intense darkness. Towards dawn the day following Quentin Dick led his companion into a wild, thickly-wooded place which seemed formed by nature as a place of refuge for a hunted creature— whether man or beast.

Entering the mouth of what seemed to be a cavern, he bade his companion wait. Presently a sound, as of the cry of some wild bird, was heard. It was answered by a similar cry in the far distance. Soon after the shepherd returned, and, taking his companion by the hand, led him into the cave which, a few paces from its mouth, was profoundly dark. Almost immediately a glimmering light appeared. A few steps farther, and Wallace found himself in the midst of an extraordinary scene.

The cavern at its inner extremity was an apartment of considerable size, and the faint light of a few lanterns showed that the place was clouded by smoke from a low fire of wood that burned at the upper end. Here, standing, seated, and reclining, were assembled all sorts and conditions of men—some in the prime and vigour of life; some bowed with the weight of years; others, both young and old, gaunt and haggard from the influence of disease and suffering, and many giving evidence by their aspect that their days on earth were numbered. Some, by the stern contraction of brow and lip, seemed to suggest that submission was the last thought that would enter their minds, but not a few of the party wore that look of patient endurance which is due to the influence of the Spirit of God—not to mere human strength of mind and will. All seemed to be famishing for want of food, while ragged clothes, shaggy beards, hollow cheeks, and unkempt locks told eloquently of the long years of bodily and mental suffering which had been endured under ruthless persecution.

# Chapter V

Immediately on entering the cave in which this party of Covenanters had found a temporary shelter, Will Wallace learned the reason of the large supply of provisions which he and his comrade had carried.

"I've brought this for ye frae Andrew Black," said Quentin, taking the wallet from his shoulder and presenting it to a man in clerical costume who advanced to welcome him. "He thought ye might stand in need o' victuals."

"Ever thoughtful of his friends; I thank him heartily," said the minister, accepting the wallet—as also that handed to him by Wallace. "Andrew is a true helper of the persecuted; and I thank the Lord who has put it into his heart to supply us at a time when our provisions are well-nigh exhausted. Our numbers have been unexpectedly increased by the arrival of some of the unfortunates recently expelled from Lanark."

"From Lanark!" echoed Wallace as he glanced eagerly round on the forlorn throng. "Can you tell me, sir, if a Mr. David Spence and a Mrs. Wallace have arrived from that quarter?"

"I have not heard of them," returned the minister, as he emptied the wallets and began to distribute their contents to those around him.—"Ah, here is milk— I'm glad our friend Black thought of that, for we have a poor dying woman here who can eat nothing solid. Here, Webster, take it to her."

With a sudden sinking at the heart Wallace followed the man to whom the milk had been given. Might not this dying woman, he thought, be his own mother? True, he had just been told that no one with her name had yet sought refuge there; but, there was a bare possibility and—anxiety does not reason! As he crossed to a spot where several persons were bending over a couch of straw, a tremendous clap of thunder shook the solid walls of the cavern. This was immediately followed by a torrent of rain, the plashing of which outside suggested that all the windows of heaven had been suddenly opened. The incident was natural enough in itself, but the anxious youth took it as a bad omen, and trembled as he had never before trembled at the disturbances of nature. One glance, however, sufficed to relieve his mind. The dying woman was young. Delicate of constitution by nature, long exposure to damp air in caves, and cold beds on the ground, with bad and insufficient food, had sealed her doom. Lying there, with hollow cheeks, eyes closed and lips deathly pale, it seemed as if the spirit had already fled.

"Oh, my ain Lizzie!" cried a poor woman who knelt beside her.

"Wheesht, mither," whispered the dying woman, slowly opening her eyes; "it is the Lord's doing—shall not the Judge of a' the earth do right? We'll understand it a' some day—for ever wi' the Lord!"

The last words were audible only to the mother's ear. Food for the body, even if it could have availed her, came too late. Another moment and she was in the land where hunger and thirst are unknown—

where the wicked cease from troubling, and the weary are at rest.

The mourners were still standing in silence gazing on the dead, when a loud noise and stamping of feet was heard at the entrance of the cave. Turning round they saw several drenched and haggard persons enter, among them a man supporting—almost carrying—a woman whose drooping figure betokened great exhaustion.

"Thank you, O thank you; I—I'm better now," said the woman, looking up with a weary yet grateful expression at her protector.

Will Wallace sprang forward as he heard the voice. "Mother! mother!" he cried, and, next moment, he had her in his arms.

The excitement coupled with extreme fatigue was almost too much for the poor woman. She could not speak, but, with a sigh of contentment, allowed her head to fall upon the broad bosom of her son.

Accustomed as those hunted people were to scenes of suffering, wild despair, and sometimes, though not often, to bursts of sudden joy, this incident drew general attention and sympathy—except, indeed, from the mother of the dead woman, whose poor heart was for the moment stunned. Several women—one of whom was evidently a lady of some position—crowded to Will's assistance, and conveyed Mrs. Wallace to a recess in the cave which was curtained off. Here they gave her food, and changed her soaking garments. Meanwhile her brother, David Spence—a grand-looking old man of gentle manners and refined mind—gave his nephew an account of the manner in which they had been driven from their home.

"What is the matter with your hands, uncle?" asked Will, observing that both were bandaged.

"They tried the thumbscrews on me," said Spence with a pitiful smile, glancing at his injured members. "They wanted to force me to sign the Bond, which I declined to do—first, because it required me to perform impossibilities; and, second, because it was such as no Government in the world has a right to exact or freeman to sign. They were going to put the boot on me at first, but the officer in command ordered them to try the thumbscrews. This was lucky, for a man may get along with damaged thumbs, but it would have been hard to travel with crippled legs! I held out though, until the pain became so great that I couldn't help giving a tremendous yell. This seemed to touch the officer with pity, for he ordered his men to let me be. Soon afterwards your mother and I managed to give them the slip, and we came on here."

"But why came you here, uncle?" asked Will.

"Because I don't want to be taken to Edinburgh and hanged. Besides, after hearing of your temporary settlement with Black, I thought the safest place for your mother would be beside yourself."

When Wallace explained the cause of his own journey, and the condition of the district around Black's farm, the plans of David Spence had to be altered. He resolved, after consideration and prayer, to take to the mountains and remain in hiding, while Mrs. Wallace should go to Edinburgh, as already planned, and live with Mrs. Black.

"But it will never do to take her along with yourself, Will," said Spence. "She cannot walk a step farther. We must try to get her a horse, and let her journey along with some o' the armed bands that attended the conventicle at Skeoch Hill. They will be sure to be returning this way in a day or two."

"You are right," said the minister who has already been introduced, and who overheard the concluding remark as he came forward. "The armed men will be passing this way in a day or two, and we will take good care of your mother, young sir, while she remains with us."

"Just so," rejoined Spence. "I'll see to that; so, nephew, you and your comrade Quentin may continue your journey with easy minds. You'll need all your caution to avoid being taken up and convicted, for the tyrants are in such a state of mind just now that if a man only *looks* independent they suspect him, and there is but a short road between suspicion and the gallows now."

"Humph! we'll be as innocent-lookin' an' submissive as bairns," remarked Quentin Dick, with a grim smile on his lips and a frown on his brow that were the reverse of childlike.

Convinced that Spence's arrangement for his mother's safety was the best in the circumstances, Wallace left her, though somewhat reluctantly, in the care of the outlawed Covenanters, and resumed his journey with the shepherd after a few hours' rest.

Proceeding with great caution, they succeeded in avoiding the soldiers who scoured the country until, towards evening, while crossing a rising ground they were met suddenly by two troopers. A thicket and bend in the road had, up to that moment, concealed them from view. Level grass-fields bordered the road on either side, so that successful flight was impossible.

"Wull ye fecht?" asked Quentin, in a quick subdued voice.

"Of course I will," returned Wallace.

"Ca' canny at first, then. Be humble an' *awfu'* meek, till I say '*Noo!*'"

The troopers were upon them almost as soon as this was uttered.

"Ho! my fine fellows," exclaimed one of them, riding up to Quentin with drawn sword, "fanatics, I'll be bound. Where from and where away now?"

"We come, honoured sir, frae Irongray, an' we're gaun to Ed'nbury t' buy cattle," answered Quentin with downcast eyes.

"Indeed, oho! then you must needs have the cash wherewith to buy the cattle. Where is it?"

"In ma pooch," said the shepherd with a deprecating glance at his pocket.

"Hand it over, then, my good fellow. Fanatics are not allowed to have money or to purchase cattle nowadays."

"But, honoured sir, we're no fannyteeks. We're honest shepherds."

The lamb-like expression of Quentin Dick's face as he said this was such that Wallace had considerable difficulty in restraining an outburst of laughter, despite their critical position. He maintained his gravity, however, and firmly grasped his staff, which, like that of his companion, was a blackthorn modelled somewhat on the pattern of the club of Hercules.

"Here, Melville," said the first trooper, "hold my horse while I ease this 'honest shepherd' of his purse."

Sheathing his sword, he drew a pistol from its holster, and, handing the reins to his companion, dismounted.

"Noo!" exclaimed Quentin, bringing his staff down on the trooper's iron headpiece with a terrific thwack. Like a flash of lightning the club of Wallace rang and split upon that of the other horseman, who fell headlong to the ground.

Strong arms have seldom occasion to repeat a well-delivered blow. While the soldiers lay prone upon the road their startled horses galloped back the way they had come.

"That's unfort'nit," said Quentin. "Thae twa look like an advance-gaird, an' if so, the main body'll no be lang o' gallopin' up to see what's the maitter. It behoves us to rin!"

The only port of refuge that appeared to them as they looked quickly round was a clump of trees on a ridge out of which rose the spire of a church.

"The kirk's but a puir sanctuary nooadays," remarked the shepherd, as he set off across the fields at a quick run, "but it's oor only chance."

They had not quite gained the ridge referred to when the danger that Quentin feared overtook them. A small company of dragoons was seen galloping along the road.

"We may gain the wood before they see us," suggested Will Wallace.

"If it *was* a wud I wadna care for the sodgers," replied

his comrade, "but it's only a bit plantation. We'll jist mak' for the manse an' hide if we can i' the coal-hole or some place."

As he spoke a shout from the troopers told that they had been seen, and several of them leaving the road dashed across the field in pursuit.

Now, it chanced that at that quiet evening hour the young curate of the district, the Reverend Frank Selby, was enjoying a game of quoits with a neighbouring curate, the Reverend George Lawless, on a piece of ground at the rear of the manse. The Reverend Frank was a genial Lowlander of the muscular type. The Reverend George was a renegade Highland-man of the cadaverous order. The first was a harum-scarum young pastor with a be-as-jolly-as-you-can spirit, and had accepted his office at the recommendation of a relative in power. The second was a mean-spirited wolf in sheep's clothing, who, like his compatriot Archbishop Sharp, had sold his kirk and country as well as his soul for what he deemed some personal advantage. As may well be supposed, neither of those curates was a shining light in the ministry.

"Missed again! I find it as hard to beat you, Lawless,

as I do to get my parishioners to come to church,"
exclaimed the Reverend Frank with a good-humoured
laugh as his quoit struck the ground and, having been
badly thrown, rolled away.

"That's because you treat your quoits carelessly, as
you treat your parishioners," returned the Reverend
George, as he made a magnificent throw and ringed
the tee.

"Bravo! that's splendid!" exclaimed Selby.

"Not bad," returned Lawless. "You see, you want more
decision with the throw—as with the congregation. If
you will persist in refusing to report delinquents and
have them heavily fined or intercommuned, you must
expect an empty church. Mine is fairly full just now,
and I have weeded out most of the incorrigibles."

"I will never increase my congregation by such
means, and I have no wish to weed out the incorrigibles,"
rejoined Selby, becoming grave as he made another
and a better throw.

At that moment our fugitive shepherds, dashing
round the corner of the manse, almost plunged into
the arms of the Reverend Frank Selby. They pulled up,
panting and uncertain how to act.

"You seem in haste, friends," said the curate, with an urbane smile.

"Oot o' the fryin'-pan into the fire!" growled Quentin, grasping his staff and setting his teeth.

"If you will condescend to explain the frying-pan I may perhaps relieve you from the fire," said Selby with emphasis.

Wallace observed the tone and grasped at the forlorn hope.

"The dragoons are after us, sir," he said eagerly; "unless you can hide us we are lost!"

"If you are honest men," interrupted the Reverend George Lawless, with extreme severity of tone and look, "you have no occasion to hide—"

"But we're *not* honest men," interrupted Quentin in a spirit of almost hilarious desperation, "we're fannyteeks,—rebels,—Covenanters,—born eediots—"

"Then," observed Lawless, with increasing austerity, "you richly deserve—"

"George!" said the Reverend Frank sharply, "you are in my parish just now, and I expect you to respect my wishes. Throw your plaids, sticks, and bonnets behind that bush, my lads—well out of sight—so. Now, cast your coats, and join us in our game."

The fugitives understood and swiftly obeyed him. While they were hastily stripping off their coats Selby took his brother curate aside, and, looking him sternly in the face, said— "Now, George Lawless, if you by word or look interfere with my plans, I will give you cause to repent it to the latest day of your life."

If any one had seen the countenance of the Reverend George at that moment he would have observed that it became suddenly clothed with an air of meekness that was by no means attractive.

At the time we write of, any curate might, with the assistance of the soldiers, fine whom he pleased, and as much as he pleased, or he might, by reporting a parishioner an absentee from public worship, consign him or her to prison, or even to the gallows. But though all the curates were in an utterly false position they were not all equally depraved. Selby was one who felt more or less of shame at the contemptible part he was expected to play.

When the troopers came thundering round the corner of the manse a few minutes later, Quentin Dick, in his shirt sleeves, was in the act of making a

OUTWITTING THE TROOPERS—Page 94

beautiful throw, and Will Wallace was watching him with interest. Even the Reverend George seemed absorbed in the game, for he felt that the eyes of the Reverend Frank were upon him.

"Excuse me, gentlemen," said the officer in command of the soldiers, "did you see two shepherds run past here?"

"No," answered the Reverend Frank with a candid smile, "I saw no shepherds run past here."

"Strange!" returned the officer, "they seemed to enter your shrubbery and to disappear near the house."

"Did you see the path that diverges to the left and takes down to the thicket in the hollow?" asked Selby.

"Yes, I did, but they seemed to have passed that when we lost sight of them."

"Let me advise you to try it now," said Selby.

"I will," replied the officer, wheeling his horse round and galloping off, followed by his men.

"Now, friends, I have relieved you from the fire, as I promised," said the Reverend Frank, turning to the shepherds; "see that you don't get into the frying-pan again. Whether you deserve hanging or not is best known to yourselves. To say truth, you don't look like it, but, judging from appearance, I should think that in these times you're not unlikely to get it. On with your coats and plaids and be off as fast as you can—over the ridge yonder. In less than half-an-hour you'll be in Denman's Dean, where a regiment of cavalry would fail to catch you."

"We shall never forget you—"

"There, there," interrupted the Reverend Frank, "be off. The troopers will soon return. I've seen more than enough of hanging, quartering, and shooting to convince me that Presbytery is not to be rooted out, nor Prelacy established, by such means. Be off, I say!"

Thus urged, the fugitives were not slow to avail themselves of the opportunity, and soon were safe in Denman's Dean.

"Now, Lawless," said the Reverend Frank in a cheerful tone, "my conscience, which has been depressed of late, feels easier this evening. Let us go in to supper; and *remember* that no one knows about this incident except you—and I. So, there's no chance of its going further."

"The two rebels know it," suggested Lawless.

"No, they don't!" replied the other airily. "They have quite forgotten it by this time, and even if it should recur to memory their own interest and gratitude would seal their lips—so we're quite safe, you and I; quite safe—come along."

Our travellers met with no further interruption until they reached Edinburgh. It was afternoon when they arrived, and, entering by the road that skirts the western base of the Castle rock, proceeded towards the Grassmarket.

Pushing through the crowd gathered in that celebrated locality, Quentin and Wallace ascended the steep street named Candlemaker Row, which led and still leads to the high ground that has since been connected with the High Street by George IV. Bridge. About half-way up the ascent they came to a semicircular projection which encroached somewhat on the footway. It contained a stair which led to the interior of one of the houses. Here was the residence of Mrs. Black, the mother of our friend Andrew. The good woman was at home, busily engaged with her knitting needles, when her visitors entered.

A glance sufficed to show Wallace whence

Andrew Black derived his grave, quiet, self-possessed character, as well as his powerful frame and courteous demeanour.

She received Quentin Dick, to whom she was well known, with a mixture of goodwill and quiet dignity.

"I've brought a freend o' Mr. Black's to bide wi' ye for a wee while, if ye can take him in," said Quentin, introducing his young companion as "Wull Wallace."

"I'm prood to receive an' welcome ony freend o' my boy Andry," returned the good woman, with a slight gesture that would have become a duchess.

"Ay, an' yer son wants ye to receive Wallace's mither as weel. She'll likely be here in a day or twa. She's been sair persecooted of late, puir body, for she's a staunch upholder o' the Covenants."

There have been several Covenants in Scotland, the most important historically being the National Covenant of 1638, and the Solemn League and Covenant of 1643. It was to these that Quentin referred, and to these that he and the great majority of the Scottish people clung with intense, almost superstitious veneration; and well they might, for these Covenants—which some enthusiasts had signed with their blood—contained nearly all the principles which lend stability and dignity to a people—such as a determination to loyally stand by and "defend the King," and "the liberties and laws of the kingdom," to have before the eyes "the glory of God, the advancement of the kingdom of our Lord and Saviour Jesus Christ, the honour and happiness of the King and his posterity, as well as the safety and peace of the people; to preserve the rights and privileges of Parliament, so that arbitrary and unlimited power should never be suffered to fall into the hands of rulers, and to vindicate and maintain the liberties of the subjects in all these things which concern their consciences, persons, and estates." In short, it was a testimony for constitutional government in opposition to absolutism.

Such were the principles for which Mrs. Black contended with a resolution equal, if not superior, to that of her stalwart son; so that it was in a tone of earnest decision that she assured her visitors that nothing would gratify her more than to receive a woman who had suffered persecution for the sake o' the Master an' the Covenants. She then ushered Wallace and Quentin Dick into her little parlour—a humble but neatly kept apartment, the back window of which—a hole not much more than two feet square—commanded a view of the tombstones and monuments of Greyfriars' Churchyard.

# Chapter VI

Mrs. Black was a woman of sedate character and considerable knowledge for her station in life—especially in regard to Scripture. Like her son she was naturally grave and thoughtful, with a strong tendency to analyse, and to inquire into the nature and causes of things. Unlike Andrew, however, all her principles and her creed were fixed and well defined—at least in her own mind, for she held it to be the bounden duty of every Christian to be ready at all times to give a "reason" for the hope that is in him, as well as for every opinion that he holds. Her natural kindness was somewhat concealed by slight austerity of manner.

She was seated, one evening, plying her ever active needle, at the same small window which overlooked the churchyard. The declining sun was throwing dark shadows across the graves. A ray of it gleamed on a corner of the particular tombstone which, being built against her house, slightly encroached upon her window. No one was with the old woman save a large cat, to whom she was in the habit of addressing occasional remarks of a miscellaneous nature, as if to relieve the tedium of solitude with the fiction of intercourse.

"Ay, pussie," she said, "ye may weel wash yer face an' purr, for there's nae fear o' *you* bein' dragged before Airchbishop Sherp to hae yer thoombs screwed, or yer legs squeezed in the—"

She stopped abruptly, for heavy footsteps were heard on the spiral stair, and next moment Will Wallace entered.

"Well, Mrs. Black," he said, sitting down in front of her, "it's all settled with Bruce. I'm engaged to work at his forge, and have already begun business."

"So I see, an' ye look business-like," answered the old woman, with a very slight smile, and a significant glance at our hero's costume.

A considerable change had indeed taken place in the personal appearance of Will Wallace since his arrival in Edinburgh, for in place of the shepherd's garb, with which he had started from the "bonnie hills of Galloway," he wore the leathern apron and other habiliments of a blacksmith. Moreover his hair had been allowed to grow in luxuriant natural curls about his head, and as the sun had bronzed him during his residence with Black, and a young beard and moustache had begun to assert themselves in premature vigour, his whole aspect was that of a grand heroic edition of his former self.

"Yes, the moment I told your friend," said Wallace, "that you had sent me to him, and that I was one of those who had good reason to conceal myself from observation, he gave me a hearty shake of the hand and accepted my offer of service; all the more that, having already some knowledge of his craft, I did not require teaching. So he gave me an apron and set me to work at once. I came straight from the forge just as I left off work to see what you would think of my disguise."

"Ye'll do, ye'll do," returned Mrs. Black, with a nod of approval. "Yer face an' hands need mair washin' than my pussie gies her nose! But wheesht! I hear a fit on the stair. It'll be Quentin Dick. I sent him oot for a red herrin' or twa for supper."

As she spoke, Quentin entered with a brown paper parcel, the contents of which were made patent by means of scent without the aid of sight.

The shepherd seemed a little disconcerted at sight of a stranger, for, as Wallace stood up, the light did not fall on his face; but a second glance sufficed to enlighten him.

"No' that bad," he said, surveying the metamorphosed shepherd, "but I doot yer auld friends the dragoons wad sune see through 't—considerin' yer size an' the soond o' yer voice."

So saying he proceeded to place the red herrings on a gridiron, as if he were the recognised cook of the establishment.

Presently Bruce himself—Mrs. Black's friend the blacksmith—made his appearance, and the four were soon seated round a supper of oat-cakes, mashed potatoes, milk, and herring. For some time they discussed the probability of Wallace being recognised by spies as one who had attended the conventicle at Irongray, or by dragoons as a deserter; then, as appetite was appeased, they diverged to the lamentable state of the country, and the high-handed doings of the Privy Council.

"The Airchbishop cam' to the toon this mornin'," remarked Mrs. Black, "so there'll be plenty o' torterin' gaun on."

"I fear you're right," said Bruce, who, having sojourned a considerable time in England, had lost much of his northern language and accent. "That horrible instrument, the *boot*, was brought this very morning to my smiddy for repair. They had been so hard on some poor wretch, I suppose, that they broke part of it, but I put a flaw into its heart that will force them to be either less cruel or to come to me again for repairs!"

"H'm! if ye try thae pranks ower often they'll find it oot," said Quentin. "Sherp is weel named, and if he suspects what ye've done, ye'll get a taste of the buit yersel'."

The hatred with which by far the greater part of

the people of Scotland regarded Archbishop Sharp of Saint Andrews is scarcely a matter of wonder when the man's character and career is considered. Originally a Presbyterian, and Minister of Crail, he was sent to Court by his brethren and countrymen as their advocate and agent, and maintained there at their expense for the express purpose of watching over the interests of their church. Sharp not only betrayed his trust but went over to what might well at that time be described as "the enemy," and secretly undermined the cause which he was bound in honour to support. Finally he threw off all disguise, and was rewarded by being made Archbishop of Saint Andrews and Primate of Scotland! This was bad enough, but the new Prelate, not satisfied with the gratification of his ambition, became, after the manner of apostates, a bitter persecutor of the friends he had betrayed. Charles the Second, who was indolent, incapable and entirely given over to self-indulgence, handed over the affairs of Scotland to an unprincipled cabal of laymen and churchmen, who may be fittingly described as drunken libertines. By these men—of whom Middleton, Lauderdale, and Sharp were the chief—all the laws passed in favour of Presbytery were rescinded; new tyrannical laws such as we have elsewhere referred to were enacted and ruthlessly enforced; Prelacy was established; the Presbyterian Church was laid in ruins, and all who dared to question the righteousness of these transactions were pronounced rebels and treated as such. There was no impartial tribunal to which the people could appeal. The King, who held Presbyterianism to be unfit for a gentleman, cared for none of these things, and even if he had it would have mattered little, for those about him took good care that he should not be approached or enlightened as to the true state of affairs in Scotland.

Sharp himself devised and drafted a new edict empowering any officer or sergeant to kill on the spot any armed man whom he found returning from or going to a conventicle, and he was on the point of going to London to have this edict confirmed when his murderous career was suddenly terminated.

In the days of James the Sixth and Charles the First, the bishops, although forced on the Scottish Church and invested with certain privileges, were subject to the jurisdiction of the General Assembly, but soon after

Charles the Second mounted the throne ecclesiastical government was vested entirely in their hands, and all the ministers who refused to recognise their usurped authority were expelled.

It was in 1662 that the celebrated Act was passed by Middleton and his colleagues in Glasgow College. It provided that all ministers must either submit to the bishops or remove themselves and families out of their manses, churches, and parishes within a month. It was known as the "Drunken Act of Glasgow," owing to the condition of the legislators. Four hundred brave and true men left their earthly all at that time, rather than violate conscience and forsake God. Their example ultimately saved the nation from despotism.

The Archbishop of Saint Andrews was chief in arrogance and cruelty among his brethren. He afterwards obtained permission to establish a High Commission Court in Scotland—in other words, an Inquisition—for summarily executing all laws, acts, and orders in favour of Episcopacy and against recusants, clergy and laity. It was under this authority that all the evil deeds hitherto described were done, and of this Commission Sharp was constant president.

It may be well to remark here that the Prelacy which was so detested by the people of Scotland was not English Episcopacy, but Scotch Prelacy. It was, in truth, little better at that time than Popery disguised— a sort of confused religio-political Popery, of which system the King was self-constituted Pope, while his unprincipled minions of the council were cardinals.

No wonder, then, that at the mere mention of Sharp's name Mrs. Black shook her head sorrowfully, Bruce the blacksmith frowned darkly, and Quentin Dick not only frowned but snorted vehemently, and smote the table with such violence that the startled pussie fled from the scene in dismay.

"Save us a'! Quentin," said Mrs. Black, "ye'll surely be hanged or shot if ye dinna learn to subdue yer wrath."

"Subdue my wrath, wumman!" exclaimed the shepherd, grinding his teeth; "if ye had seen the half o' what I've seen ye wad—but ye ken 'maist naething aboot it! Gie me some mair tatties an' mulk, it'll quiet me maybe."

In order that the reader may know something of one of the things about which Mrs. Black, as well as

Quentin Dick himself, was happily ignorant at that time, we must change the scene once more to the neighbourhood of Andrew Black's cottage.

It was early in the day, and the farmer was walking along the road that led to Cluden Ford, bent on paying a visit to Dumfries, when he was overtaken by a troop of about twenty horsemen. They had ridden out of the bush and come on the road so suddenly that Black had no time to secrete himself. Knowing that he was very much "wanted," especially after the part he had played at the recent conventicle on Skeoch Hill, he at once decided that discretion was the better part of valour, and took to his heels.

No man in all the country-side could beat the stout farmer at a race either short or long, but he soon found that four legs are more than a match for two. The troopers soon gained on him, though he ran like a mountain hare. Having the advantage, however, of a start of about three hundred yards, he reached the bend in the road where it begins to descend towards the ford before his pursuers overtook him. But Andrew felt that the narrow strip of wood beside which he was racing could not afford him shelter and that the ford would avail him nothing. In his extremity he made up his mind to a desperate venture.

On his right an open glade revealed to him the dark gorge through which the Cluden thundered. The stream was in flood at the time, and presented a fearful aspect of seething foam mingled with black rocks, as it rushed over the lynn and through its narrow throat below. A path led to the brink of the gorge which is now spanned by the Routen Bridge. From the sharp-edged cliff on one side to the equally sharp cliff on the other was a width of considerably over twenty feet. Towards this point Andrew Black sped. Close at his heels the dragoons followed, Glendinning, on a superb horse, in advance of the party. It was an untried leap to the farmer, who nevertheless went at it like a thunderbolt and cleared it like a stag. The troopers behind, seeing the nature of the ground, pulled up in time, and wheeling to the left, made for the ford. Glendinning, however, was too late. The reckless sergeant, enraged at being so often baulked by the farmer, had let his horse go too far. He tried to pull up but failed. The effort to do so rendered a leap impossible. So near was he to the fugitive that the latter was yet in the midst of his bound when the former went over the precipice; head foremost, horse and all. The poor steed fell on the rocks below and broke his neck, but the rider was shot into the deep dark pool round which the Cluden whirled in foam-flecked eddies. In the midst of its heaving waters he quickly arose flinging his long arms wildly about, and shouting for help with bubbling cry.

The iron helm, jack-boots, and other accoutrements of a seventeenth century trooper were not calculated to assist flotation. Glendinning would have terminated his career then and there if the flood had not come to his aid by sweeping him into the shallow water at the lower end of the pool, whence some of his men soon after rescued him. Meanwhile, Andrew Black, plunging into the woods on the opposite side of the river, was soon far beyond the reach of his foes.

But escape was not now the chief anxiety of our farmer, and selfishness formed no part of his character. When he had left home, a short time before, his niece Jean was at work in the dairy, Ramblin' Peter was attending to the cattle, Marion Clark and her comrade, Isabel Scott were busy with domestic affairs, and old Mrs. Mitchell—who never quite recovered her reason—was seated in the chimney corner calmly knitting a sock.

To warn these of their danger was now the urgent duty of the farmer, for well he knew that the disappointed soldiers would immediately visit his home. Indeed, he saw them ride away in that direction soon afterwards, and started off to forestall them if possible by taking a short cut. Glendinning had borrowed the horse of a trooper and left the dismounted man to walk after them.

But there was no particularly short cut to the cottage, and in spite of Andrew's utmost exertions the dragoons arrived before him. Not, however, before the wary Peter had observed them, given the alarm, got all the inmates of the farm—including Mrs. Mitchell—down into the hidy-hole and established himself in the chimney corner with a look of imbecile innocence that was almost too perfect.

Poor Peter! his heart sank when the door was flung violently open and there entered a band of soldiers, among whom he recognised some of the party which he had so recently led into the heart of a morass and so suddenly left to find their way out as they best could.

But no expression on Peter's stolid countenance betrayed his feelings.

"So, my young bantam cock," exclaimed a trooper, striding towards him, and bending down to make sure, "we've got hold of you at last?"

"Eh?" exclaimed Peter interrogatively.

"You're a precious scoundrel, aren't you?" continued the trooper.

"Ay," responded Peter.

"I told you the lad was an idiot," said a comrade. The remark was not lost upon the boy, whose expression immediately became still more idiotic if possible.

"Tell me," said Glendinning, grasping Peter savagely by one ear, "where is your master?"

"I dinna ken, sir."

"Is there nobody in the house but you?"

"Naebody but me," said Peter, "an' *you*," he added, looking vacantly round on the soldiers.

"Now, look 'ee here, lad, I'm not to be trifled with," said the sergeant. "Where are the rest of your household hidden? Answer; quick."

Peter looked into the sergeant's face with a vacant stare, but was silent. Glendinning, whose recent misfortune had rendered him unusually cruel, at once knocked the boy down and kicked him; then lifting him by the collar and thrusting him violently into the chair, repeated the question, but received no answer.

Changing his tactics he tried to cajole him and offered him money, but with similar want of success.

"Hand me your sword-belt," cried the sergeant to a comrade.

With the belt he thrashed Peter until he himself grew tired, but neither word nor cry did he extract, and, again flinging him on the floor, he kicked him severely.

"Here's a rope, sergeant," said one of the men at this point, "and there's a convenient rafter. A lad that won't speak is not fit to live."

"Nay, hanging is too good for the brute," said Glendinning, drawing a pistol from his belt. "Tie a cloth over his eyes."

Peter turned visibly paler while his eyes were being bandaged, and the troopers thought that they had at last overcome his obstinacy, but they little knew the heroic character they had to deal with.

"Now," said the sergeant, resting the cold muzzle

of his weapon against the boy's forehead, "at the word three your brains are on the floor if you don't tell me where your people are hid—one—two—"

"Stop, sergeant, let him have a taste of the thumbscrews before you finish him off," suggested one of the men.

"So be it—fetch them."

The horrible instrument of torture was brought. It was constantly used to extract confession from the poor Covenanters during the long years of persecution of that black period of Scottish history. Peter's thumbs were placed in it and the screw was turned. The monsters increased the pressure by slow degrees, repeating the question at each turn of the screw. At first Peter bore the pain unmoved, but at last it became so excruciating that his cheeks and lips seemed to turn grey, and an appalling shriek burst from him at last.

Talk of devils! The history of the human race has proved that when men have deliberately given themselves over to high-handed contempt of their Maker there is not a devil among all the legions in hell who could be worse: he might be cleverer, he could not be more cruel. The only effect of the shriek upon

Glendinning was to cause him to order another turn of the screw.

Happily, at the moment the shriek was uttered Andrew Black arrived, and, finding the troop-horses picketed outside, with no one apparently to guard them, he looked in at the window and saw what was going on.

With a fierce roar of mingled horror, surprise, and rage, he sprang into the room, and his huge fist fell on the brow of Glendinning like the hammer of Thor. His left shot full into the face of the man who had worked the screws, and both troopers fell prone upon the floor with a crash that shook the building. The act was so quick, and so overpoweringly violent that the other troopers were for a moment spellbound. That moment sufficed to enable Black to relieve the screws and set Peter free.

"C'way oot, lad, after me!" cried Andrew, darting through the doorway, for he felt that without more space to fight he would be easily overpowered. The dragoons, recovering, darted after him. The farmer caught up a huge flail with which he was wont to thresh out his oats. It fell on the headpiece of the first trooper, causing it to ring like an anvil, and stretching its owner on the ground. The second trooper fared no better, but the head of the flail broke into splinters on his iron cap, and left Andrew with the stump only to continue the combat. This, however, was no insignificant weapon, and the stout farmer laid about him with such fierce rapidity as to check for a few moments the overwhelming odds against him. Pistols would certainly have been used had not Glendinning, recovering his senses, staggered out and shouted, "Take him *alive*, men!" This was quickly done, for two troopers leaped on Andrew behind and pinioned his arms while he was engaged with four in front. The four sprang on him at the same instant. Even then Andrew Black's broad back—which was unusually "up"—proved too strong for them, for he made a sort of plunging somersault and carried the whole six along with him to the ground. Before he could rise, however, more troopers were on the top of him. Samson himself would have had to succumb to the dead weight. In a few seconds he was bound with ropes and led into the house. Ramblin' Peter had made a bold assault on a dragoon at the beginning of the fray, but could do nothing with his poor maimed hands, and was easily secured.

"Let him taste the thumbscrews," growled Glendinning savagely, and pointing to Black.

"Dae yer warst, ye born deevil," said Black recklessly— for oppression driveth even a wise man mad.

"Very good—fetch the boot," said the sergeant.

The instrument of torture was brought and affixed to the farmer's right leg; the wedge was inserted, and a blow of the mallet given.

Black's whole visage seemed to darken, his frowning brows met, and his lips were compressed with a force that meant endurance unto the death.

At that moment another party of dragoons under Captain Houston galloped up, the captain entered, and, stopping the proceedings of his subordinate, ordered Black and Peter to be set on horseback and bound together.

"Fire the place," he added. "If there are people in it anywhere, that will bring them out."

"Oh dear!" gasped Peter, "the hidy—"

"Wheesht, bairn," said Black in a low voice. "They're safe enough. The fire'll no' touch them, an' besides, they're in the Lord's hands."

A few minutes more and the whole farm-steading was in flames. The dragoons watched the work of destruction until the roof of the cottage fell in; then, mounting their horses, they descended to the road with the two prisoners and turned their faces in the direction of Edinburgh.

# Chapter VII

One day, about a week after the burning of Black's farm, a select dinner-party of red-hot rebels—as Government would have styled them; persecuted people as they called themselves—assembled in Mrs. Black's little room in Candlemaker Row. Their looks showed that their meeting was not for the purpose of enjoyment. The party consisted of Mrs. Black, Mrs. Wallace, who had reached Edinburgh in company with her brother David Spence, Jean Black, Will Wallace, Quentin Dick, and Jock Bruce the blacksmith.

"But I canna understand, lassie," said Mrs. Black to Jean, "hoo ye werena a' roasted alive i' the hidy-hole, or suffocated at the best; an' hoo did ye ever get oot wi' the ruckle o' burning' rafters abune ye?"

"It was easy enough," answered the girl, "for Uncle Andry made the roof o' the place uncommon thick, an' there's a short tunnel leadin' to some bushes by the burn that let us oot at a place that canna be seen frae the hoose. But oh, granny, dinna ask me to speak aboot thae things, for they may be torturin' Uncle Andry at this vera moment. Are you sure it was him ye saw?" she added, turning to Bruce.

"Quite sure," replied the smith. "I chanced to be passing the Tolbooth at the moment the door opened. A party of the City Guard suddenly came out with Black in the midst, and led him up the High Street."

"I'm *sure* they'll torture him," said the poor girl, while the tears began to flow at the dreadful thought. "They stick at naethin' now."

"I think," said Will Wallace, in a tone that was meant to be comforting, "that your uncle may escape the torture, for the Archbishop does not preside at the Council to-day. I hear that he has gone off suddenly to Saint Andrews."

"That won't serve your uncle much," remarked

Bruce sternly, "for some of the other bishops are nigh as bad as Sharp, and with that raving monster Lauderdale among them they're likely not only to torture but to hang him, for he is well known, and has been long and perseveringly hunted."

In his indignation the smith did not think of the effect his foreboding might have on his friend's mother, but the sight of her pale cheeks and quivering lips was not lost upon Wallace, whose sympathies had already been stirred deeply not only by his regard for Black, but also by his pity for tender-hearted Jean.

"By heaven!" he exclaimed, starting up in a sudden burst of enthusiasm, "if you will join me, friends, I am quite ready to attempt a rescue at once."

A sort of pleased yet half-cynical smile crossed the grave visage of Quentin Dick as he glanced at the youth.

"Hoots, man! sit doon," he said quietly; "ye micht as weel try to rescue a kid frae the jaws o' a lion as rescue Andry Black frae the fangs o' Lauderdale an' his crew. But something may be dune when they're takin' him back to the Tolbooth—if ye're a' wullin' to help. We mak' full twenty-four feet amangst us, an' oor shoothers are braid!"

"I'm ready," said David Spence, in the quiet tone of a man who usually acts from principle.

"An' so am I," cried Bruce, smiting the table with the fist of a man who usually acts from impulse.

While Wallace calmed his impatient spirit, and sat down to hatch a plot with his brother conspirators, a strange scene was enacting in the Council Chamber, where the perjured prelates and peers were in the habit of practising cruelty, oppression, and gross injustice under the name of law.

They sat beside a table which was covered with books and parchments. In front of them, seated on a chair with his arms pinioned, was Andrew Black. His face was pale and had a careworn look, but he held his head erect, and regarded his judges with a look of stern resolution that seemed to exasperate them considerably. On the table lay a pair of brass-mounted thumbscrews, and beside them the strange-looking instrument of torture called the boot. In regard to these machines there is a passage in the Privy Council Records which gives an idea of the spirit of the age about which we write. It runs thus: "Whereas the *boots* were the ordinary way to explicate matters relating to the Government, and there is now a new invention and engine called the *Thumbkins*, which will be very effectual to the purpose aforesaid, the Lords ordain that when any person shall by their order be put to the torture, the said boots and thumbkins be applied to them, as it shall be found fit and convenient."

Lauderdale on this occasion found it fit and convenient to apply the torture to another man in the presence of Black, in order that the latter might fully appreciate what he had to expect if he should remain contumacious. The poor man referred to had not been gifted with a robust frame or a courageous spirit. When asked, however, to reveal the names of some comrades who had accompanied him to a field-preaching he at first loyally and firmly refused to do so. Then the boot was applied. It was a wooden instrument which enclosed the foot and lower limb of the victim. Between it and the leg a wedge was inserted which, when struck repeatedly, compressed the limb and caused excruciating agony. In some cases this torture was carried so far that it actually crushed the bone, causing blood and marrow to spout forth. It was so in

the case of that well-known martyr of the Covenant,
Hugh McKail, not long before his execution.

The courage of the poor man of whom we now
write gave way at the second stroke of the mallet, and,
at the third, uttering a shriek of agony, he revealed, in
short gasps, the names of all the comrades he could
recall. Let us not judge him harshly until we have
undergone the same ordeal with credit! A look of
intense pity overspread the face of Andrew Black while
this was going on. His broad chest heaved, and drops
of perspiration stood on his brow. He had evidently
forgotten himself in his strong sympathy with the
unhappy martyr. When the latter was carried out, in a
half fainting condition, he turned to Lauderdale, and,
frowning darkly, said—

"Thou meeserable sinner, cheeld o' the deevil,
an' enemy o' a' righteousness, div 'ee think that
your blood-stained haund can owerturn the cause o'
the Lord?"

This speech was received with a flush of anger,
quickly followed by a supercilious smile.

"We shall see. Get the boot ready there. Now,
sir," (turning to Black), "answer promptly—Will you

subscribe the oath of the King's supremacy?"

"No—that I wull *not*. I acknowledge nae king ower my conscience but the King o' Kings. As for that perjured libertine on the throne, for whom there's muckle need to pray, I tell ye plainly that I consider the freedom and welfare o' Scotland stands higher than the supposed rights o' king and lords. Ye misca' us rebels! If ye ken the history o' yer ain country—whilk I misdoot—ye would ken that the Parliaments o' baith Scotland an' England have laid it doon, in declaration and in practice, that resistance to the exercise o' arbitrary power is *lawfu'*, therefore resistance to Chairles and you, his shameless flunkeys, is nae mair rebellion than it's rebellion in a cat to flee in the face o' a bull-doug that wants to worry her kittens. Against the tyrant that has abused his trust, an' upset oor constitution, an' broken a' the laws o' God and man, I count it to be my bounden duty to fecht wi' swurd an' lip as lang's I hae an airm to strike an' a tongue to wag. Noo, ye may dae yer warst!"

At a signal the executioner promptly fitted the boot to the bold man's right leg.

Black's look of indignant defiance passed away,

and was replaced by an expression of humility that, strangely enough, seemed rather to intensify than diminish his air of fixed resolve. While the instrument of torture was being arranged he turned his face to the Bishop of Galloway, who sat beside Lauderdale silently and sternly awaiting the result, and with an almost cheerful air and quiet voice said—

"God has, for His ain wise ends, made the heart o' the puir man that has just left us tender, an' He's made mine teuch, but tak' notice, thou wolf in sheep's clothing, that it's no upon its teuchness but upon the speerit o' the Lord that I depend for grace to withstand on this evil day."

"Strike!" said the Duke, in a low stern voice.

The mallet fell; the wedge compressed the strong limb, and Andrew compressed his lips.

"Again!"

A second time the mallet fell, but no sign did the unhappy man give of the pain which instantly began to shoot through the limb. After a few more blows the Duke stayed the process and reiterated his questions, but Black took no notice of him whatever. Large beads of sweat broke out on his brow. These were the only visible signs of suffering, unless we except the deathly pallor of his face.

"Again!" said the merciless judge.

The executioner obeyed, but the blow had been barely delivered when a loud snap was heard, and the tortured man experienced instant relief. Jock Bruce's little device had been successful, the instrument of torture was broken!

"Thanks be to Thy name, O God, for grace to help me thus far," said Black in a quiet tone.

"Fix on the other boot," cried Lauderdale savagely, for the constancy as well as the humility of the martyr exasperated him greatly.

The executioner was about to obey when a noise was heard at the door of the Council Chamber, and a cavalier, booted and spurred and splashed with mud, as if he had ridden fast and far, strode hastily up to the Duke and whispered in his ear. The effect of the whisper was striking, for an expression of mingled surprise, horror, and alarm overspread for a few moments even his hard visage. At the same time the Bishop of Galloway was observed to turn deadly pale, and an air of consternation generally marked the members of Council.

"Murdered—in cold blood!" muttered the Duke, as if he could not quite believe the news,—and perhaps realised for the first time that there were others besides the Archbishop of Saint Andrews who richly deserved a similar fate.

Hastily ordering the prisoner to be removed to the Tolbooth, he retired with his infamous companions to an inner room.

The well-known historical incident which was thus announced shall receive but brief comment here. There is no question at all as to the fact that Sharp was unlawfully killed, that he was cruelly slain, without trial and without judicial condemnation, by a party of Covenanters. Nothing justifies illegal killing. The justice of even legal killing is still an unsettled question, but one which does not concern us just now. We make no attempt to defend the deed of those men. It is not probable that any average Christian, whether in favour of the Covenanters or against them, would justify the killing of an old man by illegal means, however strongly he might hold the opinion that the old man deserved to die. In order to form an unprejudiced opinion on this subject recourse must be had to facts.

The following are briefly the facts of the case.

A merchant named William Carmichael, formerly a bailie of Edinburgh, was one of Sharp's favourites, and one of his numerous commissioners for suppressing conventicles in Fife. He was a licentious profligate, greedy of money, and capable of undertaking any job, however vile. This man's enormities were at last so unbearable that he became an object of general detestation, and his excessive exactions had ruined so many respectable lairds, owners, and tenants, that at last nine of these (who had been outlawed, interdicted the common intercourse of society, and hunted like wild beasts on the mountains) resolved, since all other avenues of redressing their unjust sufferings were denied them, to take the law into their own hands and personally chastise Carmichael. Accordingly, hearing that the commissioner was hunting on the moors in the neighbourhood of Cupar, they rode off in search of him. They failed to find him, and were about to disperse, when a boy brought intelligence that the coach of Archbishop Sharp was approaching.

Baffled in their previous search, and smarting under the sense of their intolerable wrongs, the party regarded this as a providential deliverance of their arch-enemy into their hands. Here was the chief cause of all their woes, the man who, more almost than any other, had been instrumental in the persecution and ruin of many families, in the torture and death of innumerable innocent men and women, and the banishment of some of their nearest and dearest to perpetual exile on the plantations, where they were treated as slaves. They leaped at the sudden and unexpected opportunity. They reasoned that what had been done in the past, and was being done at the time, would continue to be done in the future, for there was no symptom of improvement, but rather of increasing severity in the Government and ecclesiastics. Overtaking the coach, which contained the Prelate and his daughter, they stopped it, made Archbishop Sharp step out, and slew him there on Magus Moor.

It was a dark unwarrantable deed, but it was unpremeditated, and necessarily unknown, at first, to any but the perpetrators, so that it would be inexcusably unfair to saddle it upon the great body of the Covenanters, who, as far as we can ascertain from their writings and opinions, condemned it, although, naturally, they could not but feel relieved to think that one of their chief persecutors was for evermore powerless for further evil, and *some* of them refused to admit that the deed was murder. They justified it by the case of Phinehas. A better apology lies in the text, "oppression maketh a wise man mad."

This event had the effect, apparently, of causing the Council to forget our friends Black and Ramblin' Peter for a time, for they were left in the Tolbooth for about three weeks after that, whereat Andrew was much pleased, for it gave his maimed limb time to recover. As Peter remarked gravely, "it's an ill wund that blaws naebody guid!"

A robust and earnest nation cannot be subdued by persecution. The more the Council tyrannised over and trampled upon the liberties of the people of Scotland, the more resolutely did the leal-hearted and brave among them resist the oppressors. It is ever thus. It ever *should* be thus; for while an individual man has a perfect right, if he chooses, to submit to tyranny on his own account, he has no right to stand tamely by and see gross oppression and cruelty exercised towards his family, and neighbours, and country. At least, if he does so, he earns for himself the character of an unpatriotic poltroon. True patriotism consists in a readiness to sacrifice one's-self to the national well-being. As far as things temporal are concerned, the records of the Scottish Covenanters prove incontestably that those long-tried men and women submitted with unexampled patience for full eight-and-twenty years to the spoiling of their goods and the ruin of their prospects; but when it came to be a question of submission to the capricious will of the King or loyalty to Jesus Christ, thousands of them chose the latter alternative, and many hundreds sealed their testimony with their blood.

When at last the question arose, "Shall we consent to the free preaching of the Gospel being suppressed altogether, or shall we assert our rights at the point of the sword?" there also arose very considerable difference of opinion among the Covenanters. Many of those who held the peace-at-almost-any-price principle, counselled submission. Others, such as Richard Cameron, Donald Cargill, and Thomas Douglas, who believed in the right of self-defence, and in such a text as "smite a scorner and the simple will beware," advocated the use of carnal weapons for *protection alone*, although, when driven to desperation, they were compelled to go further. Some of the ejected ministers, such as Blackadder and Welsh, professed to be undecided on this point, and leant to a more or less submissive course.

Matters were now hastening to a crisis. A lawless Government had forced a law-abiding people into the appearance, though not the reality, of rebellion. The bands of armed men who assembled at conventicles became so numerous as to have the appearance of an army. The council, exasperated and alarmed, sent forth more troops to disperse and suppress these, though they had been guilty of no act of positive hostility.

At this crisis, Cargill and his friends, the "ultra-Covenanters," as they were styled, resolved to publish to the world their "Testimony to the cause and truth which they defended, and against the sins and defections of the times." They chose the 29th of May for this purpose, that being the anniversary of the King's birth and restoration. Led by Robert Hamilton, a small party of them rode into the royal burgh of

Rutherglen; and there, after burning various tyrannical Acts—as their adversaries had previously burnt the Covenants—they nailed to the cross a copy of what is now known as the Declaration of Rutherglen, in which all their grievances were set forth.

The news of this daring act spread like wildfire, and the notorious Graham of Claverhouse was sent to seize, kill, and destroy, all who took any part in this business. How Claverhouse went with his disciplined dragoons, seized John King, chaplain to Lord Cardross, with about fourteen other prisoners, in passing through Hamilton, tied them in couples, drove them before the troops like sheep, attacked the Covenanters at Drumclog, received a thorough defeat from the undisciplined "rebels," who freed the prisoners, and sent the dragoons back completely routed to Glasgow, is matter of history.

While these stirring events were going on, our friend Andrew Black and Ramblin' Peter were languishing in the unsavoury shades of the Tolbooth Prison.

One forenoon Andrew was awakened from an uneasy slumber. They bade him rise. His arms were bound with a rope, and he was led up the Canongate

towards the well-remembered Council Chamber, in
company with Ramblin' Peter, who, owing to his size
and youth, was not bound, but merely held in the
grasp of one of the guards.

At the mouth of one of the numerous closes which
lead down to the Cowgate and other parts of the old
town stood Will Wallace, Quentin Dick, David Spence,
and Jock Bruce, each armed with a heavy blackthorn.
Bruce had been warned by a friendly turnkey of what
was pending—hence their opportune presence.

As soon as the prison party was opposite the close,
the rescue party made a united rush—and the united
rush of four such strapping fellows was worth seeing.
So thought the crowd, and cheered. So thought not
the City Guard, four of whom went down like ninepins.
Black's bonds were cut and himself hurried down the
close almost before the guard had recovered from the
surprise. No doubt that guard was composed of brave
men; but when they met two such lions in the mouth
of the close as Wallace and Quentin—for these two
turned at bay—they paused and levelled their pikes.
Turning these aside like lightning the lions felled their
two foremost adversaries. The two who followed them

met a similar fate. Thinking that four were sufficient to block the entry, at least for a few moments, our heroes turned, unlionlike, and fled at a pace that soon left the enemy far behind.

This delay had given time to Black and his other friends to make good their retreat. Meanwhile Ramblin' Peter, taking advantage of the confusion, wrenched himself suddenly free from the guard who held him, and vanished down another close. The rescue having been effected, the party purposely scattered. Black's leg, however, prevented him from running fast. He therefore thought it best to double round a corner, and dash into a doorway, trusting to having been unobserved. In this, however, he was mistaken. His enemies, indeed, saw him not, but Ramblin' Peter chanced to see him while at some distance off, and made for the same place of refuge.

Springing up a spiral stair, three steps at a time, Black did not stop till he gained the attics, and leaped through the open doorway of a garret, where he found an old woman wailing over a bed on which lay the corpse of a man with a coffin beside it.

"What want ye here?" demanded the old creature angrily.

"Wow! wumman, I'm hard pressed! They're at my heels!" said Black, looking anxiously at the skylight as if meditating a still higher flight.

"Are ye ane o' the persecuted remnant?" asked the woman in a changed tone.

"Ay, that am I."

"Hide, then, hide, man—haste ye!"

"Where?" asked the perplexed fugitive. "There," said the woman, removing the coffin lid. Andrew hesitated. Just then hurrying footsteps were heard on the stair. He hesitated no longer. Stepping into the coffin he lay down, and the woman covered him up.

"Oh, wumman!" said Black, lifting the lid a little, "tak' care ye dinna meddle wi' the screw-nails. They may—"

"Wheesht! Haud yer tongue!" growled the woman sharply, and reclosed the lid with a bang, just as Ramblin' Peter burst into the room.

"What want ye here, callant?"

Peter drew back in dismay.

"I'm lookin' for—I was thinkin'—Did 'ee see a man—?"

The lid of the coffin flew off as he spoke, and his master sprang out.

"Man, Peter," gasped the farmer, "yours is the sweetest voice I've heard for mony a day. I verily thocht I was doomed—but come awa', lad. Thank 'ee kindly, auld wife, for the temporary accommodation."

The intruders left as abruptly as they had entered. That night the whole party was reassembled in Mrs. Black's residence in Candlemaker Row, where, over a supper "o' parritch an' soor mulk," Andrew Black heard from Jock Bruce all about the Declaration of Rutherglen, and the defeat of Claverhouse by the Covenanters at Drumclog.

"The thundercloods are gatherin'," said Black with a grave shake of the head, as the party broke up and were about to separate for the night. "Tak' my word for 't, we'll hear mair o' this afore lang."

We need scarcely add that on this occasion Andrew was a true prophet.

# Chapter VIII

BOTHWELL BRIDGE.

**M**atters had now come to such a pass that it was no longer possible to defer the evil day of civil war.

Persecuted inhumanly and beyond endurance, with every natural avenue of redress closed, and flushed with recent victory, the Covenanters resolved not only to hold together for defensive purposes, but to take the initiative, push their advantage, and fight for civil and religious liberty. It was the old, old fight, which has convulsed the world probably since the days of Eden—the uprising of the persecuted many against the tyrannical few. In the confusions

of a sin-stricken world, the conditions have been
occasionally and partially reversed; but, for the most
part, history's record tells of the abuse of power on
the part of the few who possess it, and the resulting
consequence that "Man's inhumanity to man,
Makes countless thousands mourn"—until the down-
trodden have turned at bay, and, like the French in
1793, have taken fearful vengeance, or, as in the case
of the Covenanters at the time of which we write, have
reaped only disaster and profounder woe.

There were, however, two elements of weakness
among the Covenanters in 1679 which rendered all
their efforts vain, despite the righteousness of their
cause. One was that they were an undisciplined body,
without appointed and experienced officers; while
their leader, Robert Hamilton, was utterly unfitted
by nature as well as training for a military command.
The other weakness was, that the unhappy differences
of opinion among them as to lines of duty, to which
we have before referred, became more and more
embittered, instead of being subordinated to the stern
necessities of the hour.

The earnest men of God amongst them could no

doubt have brought things to a better state in this crisis if their counsels had prevailed, but the men whose powers of endurance had at last given way were too many and strong for these; so that, instead of preparing for united action, the turbulent among them continued their dissensions until too late.

After Drumclog, Hamilton led his men to Glasgow to attack the enemy's headquarters there. He was repulsed, and then retired to Hamilton, where he formed a camp.

The Privy Council meanwhile called out the militia, and ordered all the heritors and freeholders to join with the Regulars in putting down the insurrection. A good many people from all quarters had joined the Covenanters after the success at Drumclog; but it is thought that their numbers never exceeded 4000. The army which prepared to meet them under the command of the Duke of Monmouth and Buccleuch was said to be 10,000 strong—among them were some of the best of the King's troops.

The Duke was anxious to delay matters, apparently with some hope of reconciliation. Many of the Covenanters were like-minded; and it is said that Mr.

Welsh visited the royal camp in disguise, with a view to a peaceful solution; but the stern spirits in both camps rendered this impossible. Some from principle, others from prejudice, could not see their way to a compromise; while the unprincipled on either side "cried havoc, and let slip the dogs of war!"

It was on Sabbath the 22nd of June that the Duke's army reached Bothwell Moor; the advanced guards entering Bothwell town within a quarter of a mile of the bridge which spans the Clyde. The Covenanters lay encamped on Hamilton Moor, on the southern side of the river.

That morning a company of stalwart young men, coming from the direction of Edinburgh, had crossed Bothwell Bridge before the arrival of the royal army and joined the Covenanters. They were preceded by two men on horseback.

"It seems a daft-like thing," said one horseman to the other as they traversed the moor, "that the likes o' me should be ridin' to battle like a lord, insteed o' trudgin' wi' the men on futt; but, man, it's no' easy to walk far efter wearin' a ticht-fittin' buit—though it was only for a wee while I had it on. It's a' verra weel for you, Wull, that's oor eleckit captain, an' can sit yer horse like a markis; but as for me, I'll slip aff an' fecht on my legs when it comes to that."

"There's no military law, Andrew, against fighting on foot," returned the captain, who, we need scarcely say, was Will Wallace; "but if you are well advised you'll stick to the saddle as long as you can. See, yonder seems to be the headquarters of the camp. We will report our arrival, and then see to breakfast."

"Ay—I'll be thankfu' for a bite o' somethin', for I'm fair famished; an' there's a proverb, I think, that says it's ill fechtin' on an emp'y stammack. It seems to me there's less order an' mair noise yonder than befits a camp o' serious men—specially on a Sabbath mornin'."

"The same thought occurred to myself," said Wallace. "Perhaps they have commenced the services, for you know there are several ministers among them."

"Mair like disputation than services," returned the farmer with a grave shake of his head.

Finding that Andrew was correct, and that the leaders of the little army were wasting the precious moments in irrelevant controversy, the Edinburgh contingent turned aside and set about preparing a hasty breakfast. This reinforcement included Quentin Dick, Jock Bruce, David Spence, and Ramblin' Peter; also Tam Chanter, Edward Gordon, and Alexander McCubine, who had been picked up on the march.

Of course, while breaking their fast they discussed the *pros* and *cons* of the situation freely.

"If the King's troops are as near as they are reported to be," said Wallace, "our chances of victory are small."

"I fear ye're richt," said Black. "It becomes Ignorance to haud its tongue in the presence o' Knowledge, nae doot—an' I confess to bein' as ignorant as a bairn o' the art o' war; but common sense seems to say that haverin' aboot theology on the eve o' a fecht is no sae wise-like as disposin' yer men to advantage. The very craws might be ashamed o' sic a noise!"

Even while he spoke a cry was raised that the enemy was in sight; and the confusion that prevailed before became redoubled as the necessity for instant action arose. In the midst of it, however, a few among the more sedate and cool-headed leaders did their best to reduce the little army to something like order, and put it in battle array. There was no lack of personal courage. Men who had, for the sake of righteousness, suffered the loss of all things, and had carried their lives in their hands for so many years, were not likely to present a timid front in the hour of battle. And leaders such as John Nisbet of Hardhill, one of the most interesting sufferers in the twenty-eight years' persecution; Clelland, who had fought with distinguished courage at Drumclog; Henry Hall of Haughhead; David Hackston of Rathillet; John Balfour of Burley; Turnbull of Bewlie; with Major Learmont and Captain John Paton of Meadowhead— two veterans who had led the Westland Covenanters in their first battle at the Pentland Hills—such men were well able to have led a band of even half-disciplined men to victory if united under a capable general. But such was not to be. The laws of God, whether relating to physics or morals, are inexorable. A divided army cannot conquer. They had assembled to fight; instead of fighting they disputed, and that so fiercely that two opposing parties were formed in the camp, and their councils of war became arenas of strife. The drilling of men had been neglected, officers were not appointed, stores of ammunition and other supplies were not provided, and no plan of battle was concerted. All this, with incapacity at the helm, resulted in overwhelming disaster and the sacrifice of a body of brave, devoted men. It afterwards intensified persecution, and postponed constitutional liberty for many years.

In this state of disorganisation the Covenanters were found by the royal troops. The latter were allowed quietly to plant their guns and make arrangements for the attack.

But they were not suffered to cross Bothwell Bridge with impunity. Some of the bolder spirits, leaving the disputants to fight with tongue and eye, drew their swords and advanced to confront the foe.

"It's every man for himsel' here," remarked Andrew Black indignantly, wiping his mouth with his cuff, as he rose from the meal which he was well aware might be his last. "The Lord hae mercy on the puir Covenanters, for they're in sair straits this day. Come awa', Wull Wallace—lead us on to battle."

Our hero, who was busily forming up his men, needed no such exhortation. Seeing that there was no one in authority to direct his movements, he resolved to act "for his own hand." He gave the word to march, and set off at a quick step for the river, where the fight had already begun. Soon he and his small band were among those who held the bridge. Here they found Hackston, Hall, Turnbull, and the lion-like John Nisbet, each with a small band of devoted followers sternly and steadily defending what they knew to be the key to their position. Distributing his men in such a way among the coppices on the river's bank that they could assail the foe to the greatest advantage without unnecessarily exposing themselves, Wallace commenced a steady fusillade on the King's foot-guards, who were attempting to storm the bridge. The Covenanters had only one cannon and about 300 men with which to meet the assault; but the gun was effectively handled, and the men were staunch.

On the central arch of the old bridge—which was long and narrow—there stood a gate. This had been closed and barricaded with beams and trees, and the parapets on the farther side had been thrown down to prevent the enemy finding shelter behind them. These arrangements aided the defenders greatly, so that for three hours the gallant 300 held the position in spite of all that superior discipline and numerous guns could do. At last, however, the ammunition of the defenders began to fail.

"Where did ye tether my horse?" asked Will Wallace, addressing Peter, who acted the part of aide-de-camp and servant to his commander.

"Ayont the hoose there," replied Peter, who was crouching behind a tree-stump.

"Jump on its back, lad, and ride to the rear at full speed. Tell them we're running short of powder and ball. We want more men, too, at once. Haste ye!"

"Ay, an' tell them frae me, that if we lose the brig we lose the day," growled Andrew Black, who, begrimed with powder, was busily loading and firing his musket from behind a thick bush, which, though an admirable screen from vision, was a poor protection from bullets, as the passage of several leaden messengers had already proved. But our farmer was too much engrossed with present duty to notice trifles!

Without a word, except his usual "Ay," Ramblin' Peter jumped up and ran to where his commander's steed was picketed. In doing so he had to pass an open space, and a ball striking his cap sent it spinning into the air; but Peter, like Black, was not easily affected by trifles. Next moment he was on the back of Will's horse—a great long-legged chestnut—and flying towards the main body of Covenanters in rear.

The bullets were whistling thickly past him. One of these, grazing some tender part of his steed's body, acted as a powerful spur, so that the alarmed creature flew over the ground at racing speed, much to its rider's satisfaction. When they reached the lines, however, and he attempted to pull up, Peter found that the great tough-mouthed animal had taken the bit in its teeth and bolted. No effort that his puny arm could make availed to check it. Through the ranks of the Covenanters he sped wildly, and in a short time was many miles from the battlefield. How long he might have continued his involuntary retreat is uncertain, but the branch of a tree brought it to a close by sweeping him off the saddle. A quarter of an hour later an old woman found him lying on the ground insensible, and with much difficulty succeeded in dragging him to her cottage.

Meanwhile the tide of war had gone against the

Covenanters. Whatever may be said of Hamilton, unquestionably he did not manage the fight well. No ammunition or reinforcements were sent to the front. The stout defenders of the bridge were forced to give way in such an unequal conflict. Yet they retired fighting for every inch of the ground. Indeed, instead of being reinforced they were ordered to retire; and at last, when all hope was gone, they reluctantly obeyed.

"Noo this bates a'!" exclaimed Black in a tone of ineffable disgust, as he ran to the end of the bridge, clubbed his musket, and laid about him with the energy of despair. Will Wallace was at his side in a moment; so was Quentin Dick. They found Balfour and Hackston already there; and for a few moments these men even turned the tide of battle, for they made an irresistible dash across the bridge, and absolutely drove the assailants from their guns, but, being unsupported, were compelled to retire. If each had been a Hercules, the gallant five would have had to succumb before such overwhelming odds. A few minutes more and the Covenanters were driven back. The King's troops poured over the bridge and began to form on the other side.

Then it was that Graham of Claverhouse, seeing his opportunity, led his dragoons across the bridge and charged the main body of the Covenanters. Undisciplined troops could not withstand the shock of such a charge. They quickly broke and fled; and now the battle was changed to a regular rout.

"Kill! kill!" cried Claverhouse; "no quarter!"

His men needed no such encouragement. From that time forward they galloped about the moor, slaying remorselessly all whom they came across.

The gentle-spirited Monmouth, seeing that the victory was gained, gave orders to cease the carnage; but Claverhouse paid no attention to this. He was like the man-eating tigers,—having once tasted blood he could not be controlled, though Monmouth galloped about the field doing his best to check the savage soldiery.

It is said that afterwards his royal father—for he was an illegitimate son of the King—found fault with him for his leniency after Bothwell. We can well believe it; for in a letter which he had previously sent to the council Charles wrote that it was "his royal will and pleasure that they should prosecute the rebels with fire and sword, and all other extremities of war." Speaking at another time to Monmouth about his conduct, Charles said, "If I had been present there should have been no trouble about prisoners." To which Monmouth replied, "If that was your wish, you should not have sent me but a *butcher*!"

In the general flight Black, owing to his lame leg, stumbled over a bank, pitched on his head, and lay stunned. Quentin Dick, stooping to succour him, was knocked down from behind, and both were captured. Fortunately Monmouth chanced to be near them at the time and prevented their being slaughtered on the spot, like so many of their countrymen, of whom it is estimated that upwards of four hundred were slain in the pursuit that succeeded the fight—many of them being men of the neighbourhood, who had not been present on the actual field of battle at all. Among others Wallace's uncle, David Spence, was killed. Twelve hundred, it is said, laid down their arms and surrendered at discretion.

Wallace himself, seeing that the day was lost and further resistance useless, and having been separated from his friends in the general *mêlée*, sought refuge in a clump of alders on the banks of the river. Another fugitive made for the same spot about the same time. He was an old man, yet vigorous, and ran well; but the soldiers who pursued soon came up and knocked him down. Having already received several dangerous wounds in the head, the old man seemed to feel that he had reached the end of his career on earth, and calmly prepared for death. But the end had not yet come. Even among the blood-stained troops of the King there were men whose hearts were not made of flint, and who, doubtless, disapproved of the cruel work in which it was their duty to take part. Instead of giving the old man the *coup de grâce*, one of the soldiers asked his name.

"Donald Cargill," answered the wounded man.

"That name sounds familiar," said the soldier. "Are not you a minister?"

"Yea, I have the honour to be one of the Lord's servants."

Upon hearing this the soldiers let him go, and bade him get off the field as fast as possible.

Cargill was not slow to obey, and soon reached the alders, where he fell almost fainting to the ground.

Here he was discovered by Wallace, and recognised as the old man whom he had met in Andrew Black's hidy-hole. The poor man could scarcely walk; but with the assistance of his stout young friend, who carefully dressed his wounds, he managed to escape. Wallace himself was not so fortunate. After leaving Cargill in a place of comparative safety, he had not the heart to think only of his own escape while uncertain of the fate of his friends. He was aware, indeed, of his uncle's death, but knew nothing about Andrew Black, Quentin Dick, or Ramblin' Peter. When, therefore, night had put an end to the fiendish work, he returned cautiously to search the field of battle; but, while endeavouring to clamber over a wall, was suddenly pounced upon by half a dozen soldiers and made prisoner.

At an earlier part of the evening he would certainly have been murdered on the spot, but by that time the royalists were probably tired of indiscriminate slaughter, for they merely bound his arms and led him to a spot where those Covenanters who had been taken prisoners were guarded.

The guarding was of the strangest and cruellest. The prisoners were made to lie flat down on the ground—

many of them having been previously stripped nearly naked; and if any of them ventured to change their positions, or raise their heads to implore a draught of water, they were instantly shot.

Next day the survivors were tied together in couples and driven off the ground like a herd of cattle. Will Wallace stood awaiting his turn, and watching the first band of prisoners march off. Suddenly he observed Andrew Black coupled to Quentin Dick. They passed closed to him. As they did so their eyes met.

"Losh, man, is that you?" exclaimed Black, a gleam of joy lighting up his sombre visage. "Eh, but I *am* gled to see that yer still leevin'!"

"Not more glad than I to see that you're not dead," responded Will quickly. "Where's Peter and Bruce?"

A stern command to keep silence and move on drowned the answer, and in another minute Wallace, with an unknown comrade-in-arms, had joined the procession.

Thus they were led—or rather driven—with every species of cruel indignity, to Edinburgh; but the jails there were already full; there was no place in which to stow such noxious animals! Had Charles the Second been there, according to his own statement, he would have had no difficulty in dealing with them; but bad as the Council was, it was not quite so brutal, it would seem, as the King.

"Put them in the Greyfriars Churchyard," was the order—and to that celebrated spot they were marched.

Seated at her back window in Candlemaker Row, Mrs. Black observed, with some surprise and curiosity, the sad procession wending its way among the tombs and round the church. The news of the fight at Bothwell Bridge had only just reached the city, and she knew nothing of the details. Mrs. Wallace and Jean Black were seated beside her knitting.

"Wha'll they be, noo?" soliloquised Mrs. Black.

"Maybe prisoners taken at Bothwell Brig," suggested Mrs. Wallace.

Jean started, dropped her knitting, and said in a low, anxious voice, as she gazed earnestly at the procession, "If—if it's them, uncle Andrew an'—an'—the others may be amang them!"

The procession was not more than a hundred yards distant—near enough for sharp, loving eyes to distinguish friends.

"I see them!" cried Jean eagerly.

Next moment she had leaped over the window, which was not much over six feet from the ground. She doubled round a tombstone, and, running towards the prisoners, got near enough to see the head of the procession pass through a large iron gate at the south-west corner of the churchyard, and to see clearly that her uncle and Quentin Dick were there—tied together. Here a soldier stopped her. As she turned to entreat permission to pass on she encountered the anxious gaze of Will Wallace as he passed. There was time for the glance of recognition, that was all. A few minutes more and the long procession had passed into what afterwards proved to be one of the most terrible prisons of which we have any record in history.

Jean Black was thrust out of the churchyard along with a crowd of others who had entered by the front gate. Filled with dismay and anxious forebodings, she returned to her temporary home in the Row.

# Chapter IX

AMONG THE TOMBS.

The enclosure at the south-western corner of Greyfriars Churchyard, which had been chosen as the prison of the men who were spared after the battle of Bothwell Bridge, was a small narrow space enclosed by very high walls, and guarded by a strong iron gate—the same gate, probably, which still hangs there at the present day.

There, among the tombs, without any covering to shelter them from the wind and rain, without bedding or sufficient food, with the dank grass for their couches and graves for pillows, did most of these unfortunates—from twelve to fifteen hundred—

live during the succeeding five months. They were
rigorously guarded night and day by sentinels who
were held answerable with their lives for the safe
keeping of the prisoners. During the daytime they
stood or moved about uneasily. At nights if any of
them ventured to rise the sentinels had orders to fire
upon them. If they had been dogs they could not have
been treated worse. Being men, their sufferings were
terrible—inconceivable. Ere long many a poor fellow
found a death-bed among the graves of that gloomy
enclosure. To add to their misery, friends were seldom
permitted to visit them, and those who did obtain
leave were chiefly females, who were exposed to the
insults of the guards.

A week or so after their being shut up here,
Andrew Black stood one afternoon leaning against
the headstone of a grave on which Quentin Dick and
Will Wallace were seated. It had been raining, and the
grass and their garments were very wet. A leaden sky
overhead seemed to have deepened their despair, for
they remained silent for an unusually long time.

"This *is* awfu'!" said Black at last with a deep sigh.
"If there was ony chance o' makin' a dash an' fechtin'

to the end, I wad tak' comfort; but to be left here to sterve an' rot, nicht an' day, wi' naethin' to do an' maist naethin' to think on—it's—it's awfu'!"

As the honest man could not get no further than this idea—and the idea itself was a mere truism—no response was drawn from his companions, who sat with clenched fists, staring vacantly before them. Probably the first stage of incipient madness had set in with all of them.

"Did Jean give you any hope yesterday?" asked Wallace languidly; for he had asked the same question every day since the poor girl had been permitted to hold a brief conversation with her uncle at the iron gate, towards which only one prisoner at a time was allowed to approach. The answer had always been the same.

"Na, na. She bids me hope, indeed, in the Lord— an' she's right there; but as for man, what can we hope frae *him*?"

"Ye may weel ask that!" exclaimed Quentin Dick, with sudden and bitter emphasis. "Man indeed! It's my opeenion that man, when left to hissel', is nae better than the deevil. I' faith, I think he's waur, for he's mair contemptible."

"Ye may be right, Quentin, for a' I ken; but some men are no' left to theirsel's. There's that puir young chiel Anderson, that was shot i' the lungs an' has scarce been able the last day or twa to crawl to the yett to see his auld mither—he's deeing this afternoon. I went ower to the tombstane that keeps the east wund aff him, an' he said to me, 'Andry, man,' said he, 'I'll no' be able to crawl to see my mither the day. I'll vera likely be deid before she comes. Wull ye tell her no' to greet for me, for I'm restin' on the Lord Jesus, an' I'll be a free man afore night, singing the praises o' redeeming love, and waitin' for *her* to come?'"

Quentin had covered his face with his hands while Black spoke, and a low groan escaped him; for the youth Anderson had made a deep impression on the three friends during the week they had suffered together. Wallace, without replying, went straight over to the tomb where Anderson lay. He was followed by the other two. On reaching the spot they observed that he lay on his back, with closed eyes and a smile resting on his young face.

"He sleeps," said Wallace softly.

"Ay, he sleeps weel," said Black, shaking his head

slowly. "I ken the look o' *that* sleep. An' yonder's his puir mither at the yett. Bide by him, Quentin, while I gang an' brek it to her."

It chanced that Mrs. Anderson and Jean came to the gate at the same moment. On hearing that her son was dead the poor woman uttered a low wail, and would have fallen if Jean had not caught her and let her gently down on one of the graves. Jean was, as we have said, singularly sympathetic. She had overheard what her uncle had said, and forthwith sat down beside the bereaved woman, drew her head down on her breast and tried to comfort her, as she had formerly tried to comfort old Mrs. Mitchell. Even the guards were softened for a few minutes; but soon they grew impatient, and ordered them both to leave.

"Bide a wee," said Jean, "I maun hae a word wi' my uncle."

She rose as she spoke, and turned to the gate.

"Weel, what luck?" asked Black, grasping both her hands through the bars.

"No luck, uncle," answered Jean, whimpering a little in spite of her efforts to keep up. "As we ken naebody o' note here that could help us, I just went straight

to the Parliament Hoose an' saw Lauderdale himsel',
but he wouldna listen to me. An' what could I say? I
couldna tell him a lee, ye ken, an' say ye hadna been
to conventicles or sheltered the rebels, as they ca' us.
But I said I was *sure* ye were sorry for what ye had done,
an' that ye would never do it again, if they would only
let you off—"

"Oh, Jean, Jean, ye're a gowk, for that was twa lees
ye telt him!" interrupted Black, with a short sarcastic
laugh; "for I'm no' a bit sorry for what I've done; an'
I'll do't ower again if ever I git the chance. Ne'er
heed, lass, you've done your best. An' hoo's mither
an' Mrs. Wallace?"

"They're baith weel; but awfu' cast doon aboot
you, an'—an'—Wull and Quentin. An'—I had maist
forgot—Peter has turned up safe an' soond. He
says that—"

"Come, cut short your haverin'," said the sentinel
who had been induced to favour Jean, partly because
of her sweet innocent face, and partly because of the
money which Mrs. Black had given her to bribe him.

"Weel, tell Peter," said Black hurriedly, "to gang
doon to the ferm an' see if he can find oot onything

aboot Marion Clerk an' Isabel Scott. I'm wae for thae lassies. They're ower guid to let live in peace at a time like this. Tell him to tell them frae me to flee to the hills. Noo that the hidy-hole is gaen, there's no' a safe hoose in a' the land, only the caves an' the peat-bogs, and even they are but puir protection."

"Uncle dear, is not the Lord our hiding-place until these calamities be overpast?" said Jean, while the tears that she could not suppress ran down her cheeks.

"Ye're right, bairn. God forgi'e my want o' faith. Rin awa' noo. I see the sentry's getting wearied. The Lord bless ye."

The night chanced to be very dark. Rain fell in torrents, and wind in fitful gusts swept among the tombs, chilling the prisoners to the very bone. It is probable that the guards would, for their own comfort, have kept a slack look-out, had not their own lives depended a good deal on their fidelity. As it was, the vigil was not so strict as it might have been; and they found it impossible to see the whole of that long narrow space of ground in so dark a night. About midnight the sentry fancied he saw three figures flitting across the yard. Putting his musket through the bars of the gate he fired at once, but could not see whether he had done execution; and so great was the noise of the wind and rain that the report of his piece was not audible more than a few paces from where he stood, except to leeward. Alarms were too frequent in those days to disturb people much. A few people, no doubt, heard the shot; listened, perchance, for a moment or two, and then, turning in their warm beds, continued their repose. The guard turned out, but as all seemed quiet in the churchyard-prison when they peered through the iron bars, they turned in again, and the sentinel recharged his musket.

Close beside one of the sodden graves lay the yet warm body of a dead man. The random bullet had found a billet in his heart, and "Nature's sweet restorer" had been merged into the sleep of death. Fortunate man! He had been spared, probably, months of slow-timed misery, with almost certain death at the end in any case.

Three men rose from behind the headstone of that grave, and looked sorrowfully on the drenched figure.

"He has passed the golden gates," said one in a low

voice. "A wonderful change."

"Ay, Wull," responsed another of the trio; "but it's noo or niver wi' us. Set yer heid agin' the wa', Quentin."

The shepherd obeyed, and the three proceeded to carry out a plan which they had previously devised—a plan which only very strong and agile men could have hoped to carry through without noise. Selecting a suitable part of the wall, in deepest shadow, where a headstone slightly aided them, Quentin planted his feet firmly, and, resting his arms on the wall, leaned his forehead against them. Black mounted on his shoulders, and, standing erect, assumed the same position. Then Wallace, grasping the garments of his friends, climbed up the living ladder and stood on Black's shoulders, so that he could just grip the top of the wall and hang on. At this point in the process the conditions were, so to speak, reversed. Black grasped Wallace with both hands by one of his ankles, and held on like a vice. The living ladder was now hanging from the top of the wall instead of standing at the foot of it, and Quentin—the lowest rung, so to speak—became the climber. From Wallace's shoulders, he easily gained the top of the wall, and was able to reach down a helping hand to Black as he made his way slowly up Wallace's back. Then both men hauled Wallace up with some trouble, for the strain had been almost too much for him, and he could hardly help himself.

At this juncture the sentinel chanced to look up, and, dark though it was, he saw the three figures on the wall a little blacker than the sky behind. Instantly the bright flash of his musket was seen, and the report, mingled with his cry of alarm, again brought out the guard. A volley revealed the three prisoners for a moment.

"Dinna jump!" cried Black, as the bullets whizzed past their heads. "Ye'll brek yer legs. Tak' it easy. They're slow at loadin'; an' 'the mair hurry the less speed!'"

The caution was only just in time, for the impulsive Wallace had been on the point of leaping from the wall; instead of doing which he assisted in reversing the process which has just been described. It was much easier, however; and the drop which Wallace had to make after his friends were down was broken by their catching him in their arms. Inexperience, however, is always liable to misfortune. The shock of such a heavy man dropping from such a height gave them a surprise, and sent them all three violently to the ground; but the firing, shouting, and confusion on the other side of the wall caused them to jump up with wonderful alacrity.

"Candlemaker Raw!" said Black in a hoarse whisper, as they dashed off in different directions, and were lost in blackness of night.

With a very sad face, on which, however, there was an air of calm resignation, Mrs. Black sat in her little room with her Bible open before her. She had been reading to Mrs. Wallace and Jean, preparatory to retiring for the night.

"It's awful to think of their lying out yonder, bedless, maybe supperless, on a night like this," said Mrs. Wallace.

Jean, with her pretty face in that condition which the Scotch and Norwegian languages expressively call begrutten, could do nothing but sigh.

Just then hurried steps were heard on the stair, and next moment a loud knocking shook the door.

"Wha's that?" exclaimed Mrs. Black, rising.

"It's me, mither. Open; quick!"

Next moment Andrew sprang in and looked hastily round.

"Am I the first, mither?"

Before the poor woman could recover from her joy and amazement sufficiently to reply, another step was heard on the stair.

"That's ane o' them," said Black, turning and holding the door, so as to be ready for friend or foe. He was right. Mrs. Wallace uttered a little scream of joy as her son leaped into the room.

"Whaur's Quentin?" asked Black.

The question was scarcely put when the shepherd himself bounded up the stair.

"They've gotten sight o' me, I fear," he said. "Have ye a garret, wummin—onywhere to hide?"

"No' a place in the hoose big enough for a moose to hide in," said Mrs. Black with a look of dismay.

As she spoke a confused noise of voices and hurrying steps was heard in the street. Another moment and they were at the foot of the stair. The three men seized the poker, tongs, and shovel. Mrs. Black opened her back window and pointed to the churchyard.

"Yer only chance!" she said.

Andrew Black leaped out at once. Wallace followed like a harlequin. Quentin Dick felt that there was no time for him to follow without being seen. Dropping his poker he sprang through the doorway, and, closing the door on himself, began to thunder against it, just as an officer leading some of the town-guard reached the landing.

"Open, I say!" cried Quentin furiously, "I'm *sure* the rebels cam in here. Dinna be keepin' the gentlemen o' the gaird waitin' here. Open, I say, or I'll drive the door in!"

Bursting the door open, as though in fulfilment of his threat, Quentin sprang in, and looking hastily round, cried, as if in towering wrath, "Whaur are they? Whaur are thae pestiferous rebels?"

"There's nae rebels here, gentlemen," said Mrs. Black. "Ye're welcome to seek."

"They maun hae gaen up the next stair," said Quentin, turning to the officer.

"And pray, who are you, that ye seem so anxious to catch the rebels?"

"Wha am I?" repeated Quentin with glaring eyes, and a sort of grasping of his strong fingers that suggested the idea of tearing some one to pieces. "Div 'ee no see that I'm a shepherd? The sufferin's than I hae gaen through an' endured on accoont o' thae rebels is past— But c'way, sirs, they'll escape us if we stand haverin' here."

So saying the bold man dashed down the stair and into the next house, followed by the town-guards, who did not know him. The prisoners' guards were fortunately searching in another direction. A strict search was made in the next house, at which Quentin assisted. When they were yet in the thick of it he went quietly down-stairs and walked away from the scene, as he expressed it, "hotchin'"—by which he meant chuckling.

But poor Andrew Black and Will Wallace were not so fortunate. A search which was made in the outer churchyard resulted in their being discovered among the tombs, and they were forthwith conducted to the Tolbooth prison.

When Ramblin' Peter, after many narrow escapes, reached the farm in Dumfries in a half-famished state, he sat down among the desolate ruins and howled with grief. Having thus relieved his feelings, he dried his eyes and proceeded in his usual sedate manner to examine things in detail. He soon found that his master had been wrong in supposing that the hidy-hole had been discovered or destroyed. As he approached the outer end of the tunnel a head suddenly appeared above ground, and as suddenly vanished.

"Hallo!" exclaimed Peter in surprise.

"Hallo!" echoed the head, and reappeared blazing with astonishment. "Is that you, Peter?"

"Ay, McCubine, that's me. I thought ye was a' deid. Hae ye ony parritch i' the hole? I'm awfu' hungry."

"C'way in, lad: we've plenty to eat here, an guid company as weel—the Lord be thankit."

The man led the way—familiar enough to Peter; and in the hidy-hole he found several persons, some of whom, from their costume, were evidently ministers. They paid little attention to the boy at first, being engaged in earnest conversation.

"No, no, Mr. Cargill," said one. "I cannot agree with you in the stern line of demarcation which you would draw between us. We are all the servants of the most high God, fighting for, suffering for, the truth as it is in Jesus. It is true that rather than bow to usurped power

I chose to cast in my lot with the ejected; but having done that, and suffered the loss of all things temporal, I do not feel called on to pronounce such absolute condemnation on my brethren who have accepted the Indulgence. I know that many of them are as earnest followers of Christ as ourselves—it may be more so—but they think it right to bow before the storm rather than risk civil war; to accept what of toleration they can get, while they hope and pray for more."

"In that case, Mr. Welsh," replied Cargill, "what comes of their testimony for the truth? Is not Christ King in his own household? Charles is king in the civil State. The oath which he requires of every minister who accepts the Indulgence distinctly recognises him—the king—as lord of the conscience, ruler of the spiritual kingdom of this land. To take such an oath is equivalent to acknowledging the justice of his pretensions."

"They do not see it in that light," returned Mr. Welsh. "I agree with your views, and think our Indulged brethren in the wrong; but I counsel forbearance, and cannot agree with the idea that it is our duty to refuse all connection with them, and treat them as if they belonged to the ranks of the malignants. See what such opinions have cost us already in the overwhelming disaster at Bothwell Brig."

"Overwhelming disaster counts for nothing in such a cause as this," rejoined Cargill gravely. "The truth has been committed to us, and we are bound to be valiant for the truth—even to death. Is it not so, Mr Cameron?"

The young man to whom the old Covenanter turned was one of the most noted among the men who fought and died for the Covenant. An earnest godly young minister, he had just returned from Holland with the intention of taking up the standard which had been almost dropped in consequence of the hotter persecutions which immediately followed the battle of Bothwell Bridge.

"Of course you know that I agree with you, Mr. Cargill. When you licensed me to preach the blessed Gospel, Mr. Welsh, you encouraged me to independent thought. Under the guidance, I believe, of the Holy Spirit, I have been led to see the sinfulness of the Indulgence, and I am constrained to preach against it. Truly my chief concern is for the salvation of souls—the bringing of men and women and children to the Saviour; but after that, or rather along with that, to my mind, comes the condemnation of sin, whether public or private. Consider what the Indulgence and persecution together have done now. Have they not well-nigh stopped the field-preaching altogether, so that, with the exception of yourselves and Mr. Thomas Douglas and a few others, there is no one left to testify? Part of my mission has been to go round among the ministers on this very point, but my efforts have been in vain as far as I have yet gone. It has been prophesied," continued Cameron with a sad smile, "that I shall yet lose my head in this cause. That may well be, for there is that in my soul which will not let me stand still while my Master is dishonoured and sin is triumphant. As to the King, he may, so far as I know, be truly descended from the race of our kings, but he has so grievously departed from his duty to the people—by whose authority alone magistrates exist—and has so perjured himself, usurped authority in Church matters, and tyrannised in matters civil, that the people of Scotland do no longer owe him allegiance; and although I stand up for governments and governors, such as God's Word and our covenants allow, I will surely—with all who choose to join me— disown Charles Stuart as a tyrant and a usurper."

The discussion had continued so long that the ministers, as if by mutual consent, dropped it after this point, and turned to Ramblin' Peter, who was appeasing his hunger with a huge "luggie o' parritch." But the poor boy had no heart to finish his meal on learning that Marion Clark and Isabel Scott—of whom he was very fond—had been captured by the soldiers and sent to Edinburgh. Indeed nothing would satisfy him but that he should return to the metropolis without delay and carry the bad news to his master.

That same night, when darkness rendered it safe, Cargill, Cameron, Welsh, and Douglas, with some of their followers, left Black's place of concealment, and went off in different directions to risk, for a brief space, the shelter of a friendly cottage, where the neighbours would assemble to hear the outlawed ministers while one of them kept watch, or to fulfil their several engagements for the holding of conventicles among the secret places of the hills.

# Chapter X

FIERCER AND FIERCER.

After his escape, Quentin Dick, hearing of the recapture of his comrades, and knowing that he could not in any way help them, resolved to go back to Dumfries to make inquiries about the servant lassies Marion and Isabel, being ignorant of the fact that Ramblin' Peter had been sent on the same errand before him.

Now, although the one was travelling to, and the other from, Edinburgh, they might easily have missed each other, as they travelled chiefly at night in order to escape observation. But, hearing on the way that the much-loved minister, Mr. Welsh, was to preach in a certain locality, they both turned aside to hear him, and thus came together.

A price of 500 pounds sterling had been set on the head of Mr. Welsh, and for twenty years he had been pursued by his foes, yet for that long period he succeeded in eluding his pursuers—even though the resolute and vindictive Claverhouse was among them,—and in continuing his work of preaching to the people. Though a meek and humble man, Welsh was cool, courageous, and self-possessed, with, apparently, a dash of humour in him—as was evidenced by his preaching on one occasion in the middle of the frozen Tweed, so that either he "might shun giving offence to both nations, or that two kingdoms might dispute his crime!"

The evening before the meeting at which Quentin and Peter unwittingly approached each other, Mr. Welsh found himself at a loss where to spend the night, for the bloodhounds were already on his track. He boldly called at the house of a gentleman who was personally unknown to him, but who was known to be hostile to field-preachers in general, and to himself in particular. As a stranger Mr. Welsh was kindly received. Probably in such dangerous times it was considered impolite to make inquiry as to names. At all events the record says that he remained unknown. In course of conversation his host referred to Welsh and the difficulty of getting hold of him.

"I am sent," said Welsh, "to *apprehend rebels*. I know where Mr. Welsh is to preach to-morrow, and will give you the rebel by the hand."

Overjoyed at this news the gentleman agreed to accompany him to the meeting on the morrow. Arriving next day at the rendezvous, the congregation made way for the minister and his host. The latter was then invited to take a seat, and, to his great amazement, his guest of the previous night stood up and preached. At the close of the sermon Mr. Welsh held out his hand to his host.

"I promised," he said, "to give you Mr. Welsh by the hand."

"Yes," returned the gentleman, who was much affected, as he grasped the hand, "and you said that you were sent to apprehend rebels. Let me assure you that I, a rebellious sinner, have been apprehended this day."

It was at this interesting moment that Quentin

and Peter recognised each other, and, forgetting all other points of interest, turned aside to discuss their own affairs.

"Then there's nae use o' my gaun ony farer," said the shepherd thoughtfully.

"Nane whatever," said Peter; "ye'd best c'way back t' toon wi' me. Ye'll be safer there nor here, an' may chance to be o' service to the lassies."

Alas for the poor lassies! They were in the fangs of the wolves at that very time. In that council-room where, for years, the farce of "trial" and the tragedy of cruel injustice had been carried on, Marion Clark and Isabel Scott were standing before their civil and clerical inquisitors. The trial was nearly over. Proceeding upon their mean principle of extracting confession by the method of entrapping questions, and thus obtaining from their unsuspecting victims sufficient evidence— as they said—to warrant condemnation, they had got the poor serving-maids to admit that they had attended field-preachings; had conversed with some whom the Government denounced as rebels; and other matters which sufficed to enable them to draw up a libel. Those two innocent girls were then handed over to the Justiciary Court, before which they were charged with the crime of receiving and corresponding with Mr. Donald Cargill, Mr. Thomas Douglas, Mr. John Welsh, and Mr. Richard Cameron; with the murderers of Archbishop Sharp; and with having heard the said ministers preach up treason and rebellion!

When the indictment was read to them the poor things meekly admitted that it was correct, except in so far as it called the ministers rebels and asserted that they preached up treason. The jury were exceedingly unwilling to serve on the trial, but were compelled to do so under threat of fine. After deliberating on the evidence they found the girls both guilty, by their own confession, of holding the opinions charged against them, but that as actors, or receivers of rebels, the charge was not proven.

Upon this they were condemned to die, but before leaving the court Isabel Scott said impressively: "I take all witness against another at you to your appearance before God, that your proceeding against us this day is only for owning Christ, His Gospel, and His members."[1]

---

1. See *A Cloud of Witnesses*, p. 122 (ed. 1871.)

They were then led back to prison.

When Quentin and Peter arrived in Edinburgh, two days later, they passed under the West Port, which was decorated with the shrivelled heads and hands of several martyrs, and made their way to the Grassmarket, which they had to traverse in going towards Candlemaker Row. Here they found a large crowd surrounding the gallows-tree which did such frequent service there. Two female figures were swinging from the beam.

"The auld story," said the shepherd in a low sad voice. "What was their crime?" he inquired of a bystander.

"They tried to serve the Lord, that was a'," replied the man bitterly. "But they ended their coorse bravely. Ane sang the 84th Psalm and the ither spake of God's great love an' free grace to her and to sinfu' man."

"Puir things!" exclaimed Quentin with tremulous voice. "It's ower noo. They're fairly inside o' the celestial gates."

The sight was all too common in those dark days to induce delay, but the two friends had to pass near the gallows, and naturally looked up in passing.

"Quentin!" gasped Peter, stretching out both hands towards the martyrs, whose now soulless frames were hanging there, "it's—it's Marion an'—"

A low wail followed, as the poor boy fell over in a swoon.

The shepherd's heart almost stood still, and his great chest quivered for a moment as he gazed, but he was a man of strong will and iron mould. Stooping, he picked up his little friend and carried him silently away.

Their grief was, however, diverted to other channels on reaching the abode of Mrs. Black, for there they found her and Mrs. Wallace and Jean in deepest sorrow over the terrible news just brought to them by Jock Bruce.

Andrew Black, he told them, had been sent a prisoner to the Bass Rock, and Will Wallace, with two hundred others, had been banished to the plantations in Barbadoes, where they were to be sold as slaves.

Quentin sat down, covered his face with both hands, and groaned aloud on hearing this. Peter, who had recovered by that time, looked about him with the expressionless face of one whose reason has been unseated. Observing that Jean was sitting apart, sobbing as if her heart would break, he went quietly to her, and, taking one of her hands, began to stroke it gently. "Dinna greet, Jean," he said; "the Lord will deliver them. Marion aye telt me that, an' I believe she was richt."

Truly these unfortunate people needed all the consolation that the Word could give them, for banishment to the plantations usually meant banishment for life, and as to the hundreds who found a prison on the bleak and rugged Bass Rock at the mouth of the Forth, many of these also found a grave.

After the battle of Bothwell Bridge the persecutions which had been so severe for so many years were continued with intensified bitterness. Not only were all the old tyrannical laws carried into force with increased severity, but new and harsher laws were enacted. Among other things the common soldiers were given the right to carry these laws into effect—in other words, to murder and plunder according to their own will and pleasure. And now, in 1680, began what has been termed *the killing-time*, in which Graham of

Claverhouse (afterwards Viscount Dundee), Grierson of Lagg, Dalziel, and others, became pre-eminently notorious for their wanton cruelty in slaughtering men, women, and even children.

On 22nd June 1680 twenty armed horsemen rode up the main street of the burgh of Sanquhar. The troop was headed by Richard Cameron and his brother Michael, who, dismounting, nailed to the cross a paper which the latter read aloud. It was the famous "Declaration of Sanquhar," in which Charles Stuart was publicly disowned.

While the fields of Scotland were being traversed and devastated by a lawless banditti, authorised by a lawless and covenant-breaking king and Government, those indomitable men who held with Cameron and Cargill united themselves more closely together, and thus entered into a new bond pledging themselves to be faithful to God and to each other in asserting their civil and religious rights, which they believed could only be secured by driving from the throne that "perfidious covenant-breaking race, untrue both to the most high God and to the people over whom for their sins they were set."

If the Cameronians were wrong in this opinion then must the whole nation have been wrong, when, a few years later, it came to hold the same opinion, and acted in accordance therewith! As well might we find fault with Bruce and Wallace as with our covenanting patriots.

Be this as it may, Richard Cameron with his followers asserted the principle which afterwards became law— namely, that the House of Stuart should no longer desecrate the throne. He did not, however, live to see his desire accomplished.

At Airsmoss—in the district of Kyle—with a band of his followers, numbering twenty-six horse and forty foot, he was surprised by a party of upwards of one hundred and twenty dragoons under command of Bruce of Earlshall. The Cameronians were headed by Hackston of Rathillet, who had been present at the murder of Sharp, though not an active participator. Knowing that no mercy was to be expected they resolved to fight. Before the battle Cameron, engaging in a brief prayer, used the remarkable words: "Lord, take the ripe, but spare the green." The issue against such odds was what might have been expected. Nearly all the Covenanters were slain. Richard Cameron fell, fighting back to back with his brother. Some of the foot-men escaped into the moss. Hackston was severely wounded and taken prisoner. Cameron's head and hands were cut off and taken to Edinburgh, where they were cruelly exhibited to his father—a prisoner at the time. "Do ye know them?" asked the wretch who brought them. The old man, kissing them, replied, "Ay, I know them! They are my son's—my own dear son's! It is the Lord; good is the will of the Lord, who cannot wrong me nor mine, but has made goodness and mercy to follow us all our days." A wonderful speech this from one suffering under, perhaps, the severest trial to which poor human nature can be subjected. Well might be applied to him the words—slightly paraphrased—"O man, great was thy faith!"

Hackston was taken to Edinburgh, which he entered on a horse with his head bare and his face to the tail, the hangman carrying Cameron's head on a halter before him. The indignities and cruelties which were perpetrated on this man had been minutely pre-arranged by the Privy Council. We mention a few in order that the reader may the better understand the inconceivable brutality of the Government against which the Scottish Covenanters had to contend. Besides the barbarities connected with poor Cameron's head and hands, it was arranged that Hackston's body was to be drawn backward on a hurdle to the cross of Edinburgh, where, in the first place, his right hand was to be struck off, and after some time his left hand. Thereafter he was to be hanged up and cut down alive; his bowels to be taken out and his heart shown to the people by the hangman, and then to be burnt in a fire on the scaffold. Afterwards his head was to be cut off, and his body, divided into four quarters, to be sent respectively to Saint Andrews, Glasgow, Leith, and Burntisland.

In carrying out his fiendish instructions the bungling executioner was a long time mangling the wrist of Hackston's right arm before he succeeded in separating the hand. Hackston quietly advised him to be more careful to strike in the joint of the left. Having been drawn up and let fall with a jerk, three times, life was not extinct, for it is said that when the heart was torn out it moved after falling on the scaffold.

Several others who had been with Cameron were

betrayed at this time, by apostate comrades, tried under torture, and executed; and the persecution became so hot that field-preaching was almost extinguished. The veteran Donald Cargill, however still maintained his ground.

This able, uncompromising, yet affectionate and charitable man had prepared a famous document called the "Queensferry Paper," of which it has been said that it contains "the very pith of sound constitutional doctrine regarding both civil and ecclesiastical rights." Once, however, he mistook his mission. In the presence of a large congregation at Torwood he went so far as to excommunicate Charles the Second; the Dukes of York, Lauderdale, and Rothes; Sir C McKenzie and Dalziel of Binns. That these despots richly deserved whatever excommunication might imply can hardly be denied, but it is equally certain that prolonged and severe persecution had stirred up poor Cargill upon this occasion to overstep his duty as a teacher of love to God and man.

Heavily did Cargill pay for his errors—as well as for his long and conscientious adherence to duty. Five thousand merks were offered for him, dead or alive.

Being captured, he was taken to Edinburgh on the 15th of July, and examined by the Council. On the 26th he was tried and condemned, and on the 27th he was hanged, after having witnessed a good confession, which he wound up with the words: "I forgive all men the wrongs they have done against me. I pray that the sufferers may be kept from sin and helped to know their duty."

About this time a *test* oath was ordered to be administered to all men in position or authority. The gist of it was that King Charles the Second was the only supreme governor in the realm over all causes, as well ecclesiastical as civil, and that it was unlawful for any subject upon pretence of reformation, or any pretence whatever, to enter into covenants or leagues, or to assemble in any councils, conventicles, assemblies, etc., ecclesiastical or civil, without his special permission.

Pretty well this for a king who had himself signed the covenant—without which signing the Scottish nation would never have consented to assist in putting him on the throne! The greater number of the men in office in Scotland took the oath, though there were several exceptions—the Duke of Argyll, the Duke of

Hamilton, John Hope of Hopetoun, the Duchess of Rothes, and others—among whom were eighty of the conforming clergy whose loyalty could not carry them so far, and who surrendered their livings rather than their consciences.

It would require a volume to record even a bare outline of the deeds of darkness that were perpetrated at this time. We must dismiss it all and return to the actors in our tale.

Will Wallace, after being recaptured, as already stated, was sent off to the plantations in a vessel with about two hundred and fifty other unfortunates, many of whom were seriously ill, if not dying, in consequence of their long exposure in the Greyfriars' Churchyard. Packed in the hold of the ship so closely that they had not room to lie down, and almost suffocated with foul air and stench, the sufferings which they endured were far more terrible than those they experienced when lying among the tombs; but God sent most of them speedy deliverance. They were wrecked on the coast of Orkney. At night they were dashed on the rocks. The prisoners entreated to be let out of their prison, but the brutal captain ordered the hatches to be chained down. A tremendous wave cleft the deck, and a few of the more energetic managed to escape and reach the shore. The remainder—at least two hundred—were drowned in the hold. Will Wallace was among the saved, but was taken to Leith and transferred to another vessel. After several months of tossings on the deep he reached his destination and was sold into slavery.

Many months—even years—passed away, but no news reached Candlemaker Row regarding the fate of the banished people. As to Andrew Black, the only change that took place in his condition during his long captivity was his transference—unknown to his kindred—from the gloomy prison of the Bass Rock to the still gloomier cells of Dunnottar Castle.

During all this time, and for some years after, the persecutions were continued with ever-increasing severity: it seemed as if nothing short of the extirpation of the Covenanters altogether was contemplated. In short, the two parties presented at this period an aspect of human affairs which may well be styled monstrous. On the one hand a people suffering and fighting to the death to uphold law, and on the other a tyrant king and arrogant ecclesiastics and nobles, with their paid slaves and sycophants, deliberately violating the same!

Quentin Dick and Ramblin' Peter had been drawn closer together by powerful sympathy after the imprisonment of Black and the banishment of Will Wallace. They were like-minded in their aspirations, though very dissimilar in physical and mental endowment. Feeling that Edinburgh was not a safe place in which to hide after his recent escape, Quentin resolved to return to Dumfries to inquire after, and if possible to aid, his friends there.

Peter determined to cast in his lot with him. In size he was still a boy though he had reached manhood.

"We maun dae our best to help the wanderers" said the shepherd, as they started on their journey.

"Ay," assented Peter.

Arrived in Galloway they were passing over a wide moorland region one afternoon when a man suddenly appeared before them, as if he had dropped from the clouds, and held out his hand.

"What! McCubine, can that be you?" exclaimed Quentin, grasping the proffered hand. "Man, I *am* glad to see ye. What brings ye here?"

McCubine explained that he and his friend Gordon, with four comrades, were hiding in the Moss to avoid a party of dragoons who were pursuing them. "Grierson of Lagg is with them, and Captain Bruce is in command," he said, "so we may expect no mercy if they catch us. Only the other day Bruce and his men dragged puir old Tam McHaffie out o' his bed, tho' he was ill wi' fever, an' shot him."

Having conducted Quentin and Peter to the secret place where his friends were hidden, McCubine was asked anxiously, by the former, if he knew anything about the Wilsons.

"Ay, we ken this," answered Gordon, "that although the auld folk have agreed to attend the curates for the sake o' peace, the twa lassies have refused, and been driven out o' hoose an' hame. They maun hae been wanderin' amang the hills noo for months—if they're no catched by this time."

Hearing this, Quentin sprang up.

"We maun rescue them, Peter," he said.

"Ay," returned the boy. "Jean Black will expect that for Aggie's sake; she's her bosom freend, ye ken."

Refusing to delay for even half an hour, the two friends hurried away. They had scarcely left, and the six hunted men were still standing on the road where they had bidden them God-speed, when Bruce with his dragoons suddenly appeared—surprised and captured them all. With the brutal promptitude peculiar to that well-named "killing-time," four of them were drawn up on the road and instantly shot, and buried where they fell, by Lochenkit Moor, where a monument now marks their resting place.

The two spared men, Gordon and McCubine, were then, without reason assigned, bound and carried away. Next day the party came to the Cluden Water, crossing which they followed the road which leads to Dumfries, until they reached the neighbourhood of Irongray. There is a field there with a mound in it, on which grows a clump of old oak-trees. Here the two friends were doomed without trial to die. It is said that the minister of Irongray at that time was suspected of favourable leanings toward the Covenanters, and that the proprietor of the neighbouring farm of Hallhill betrayed similar symptoms; hence the selection of the particular spot between the two places, in order to intimidate both the minister and the farmer. This may well have been the case, for history shows that a very strong and indomitable covenanting spirit prevailed among the parishioners of Irongray as well as among the people of the South and West of Scotland generally. Indeed Wodrow, the historian, says that the people of Irongray were the first to offer strenuous opposition to the settlement of the curates.

When Gordon and McCubine were standing under the fatal tree with the ropes round their necks, a sorrowing acquaintance asked the latter if he had any word to send to his wife.

"Yes," answered the martyr; "tell her that I leave her and the two babes upon the Lord, and to his promise: 'A father to the fatherless and a husband to the widow is the Lord in His holy habitation.'"

Hearing this, the man employed to act the part of executioner seemed touched, and asked forgiveness.

"Poor man!" was the reply, "I forgive thee and all men."

They died, at peace with God and man. An old tombstone, surrounded by an iron rail, marks to this day the spot among the old oak-trees where the bodies of McCubine and Gordon were laid to rest.

Commenting on this to his friend Selby, the Reverend George Lawless gave it as his opinion that "two more fanatics were well out of the world."

To which the Reverend Frank replied very quietly:

"Yes, George, well out of it indeed; and, as I would rather die with the fanatics than live with the godless, I intend to join the Covenanters to-night—so my pulpit shall be vacant to-morrow."

# Chapter XI

COMING EVENTS CAST SHADOWS.

In February 1685 Charles the Second died—not without some suspicion of foul play. His brother, the Duke of York, an avowed Papist, ascended the throne as James the Second. This was a flagrant breach of the Constitution, and Argyll—attempting to avert the catastrophe by an invasion of Scotland at the same time that Monmouth should invade England—not only failed, but was captured and afterwards executed by the same instrument—the "Maiden"—with which his father's head had been cut off nigh a quarter of a century before. As might have been expected, the persecutions were not relaxed by the new king.

When good old Cargill was martyred, a handsome fair young man was looking on in profound sorrow and pity. He was a youth of great moral power, and with a large heart. His name was James Renwick. From that hour this youth cast in his lot with the persecuted wanderers, and, after the martyrdom of Cameron and Cargill, and the death of Welsh, he was left almost alone to manage their affairs. The "Strict Covenanters" had by this time formed themselves into societies for prayer and conference, and held quarterly district meetings in sequestered places, with a regular system of correspondence—thus secretly forming an organised body, which has continued down to modern times.

It was while this young servant of God—having picked up the mantle which Cargill dropped—was toiling and wandering among the mountains, morasses, and caves of the west, that a troop of dragoons was seen, one May morning, galloping over the same region "on duty." They swept over hill and dale with the dash and rattle of men in all the pride of youth and strength and the panoply of war. They were hasting, however, not to the battlefield but to the field of agriculture, there to imbrue their hands in the blood of the unarmed and the helpless.

At the head of the band rode the valiant Graham of Claverhouse. Most people at that time knew him as the "bloody Clavers," but as we look at the gay cavalier with his waving plume, martial bearing, beautiful countenance, and magnificent steed, we are tempted to ask, "Has there not been some mistake here?" Some have thought so. One or two literary men, who might have known better, have even said so, and attempted to defend their position!

"Methinks this is our quarry, Glendinning," said Claverhouse, drawing rein as they approached a small cottage, near to which a man was seen at work with a spade.

"Yes—that's John Brown of Priesthill," said the sergeant.

"You know the pestilent fanatic well, I suppose?"

"Ay. He gets the name o' being a man of eminent godliness," answered the sergeant in a mocking tone; "and is even credited with having started a Sabbath-school!"

John Brown, known as the "Christian carrier," truly was what Glendinning had sneeringly described him. On seeing the cavalcade approach he guessed, no doubt, that his last hour had come, for many a time had he committed the sin of succouring the outlawed Covenanters, and he had stoutly refused to attend the ministry of the worthless curate George Lawless. Indeed it was the information conveyed to Government by that reverend gentleman that had brought Claverhouse down upon the unfortunate man.

The dragoons ordered him to proceed to the front of his house, where his wife was standing with one child in her arms and another by her side. The usual ensnaring questions as to the supremacy of the King, etc., were put to him, and the answers being unsatisfactory, Claverhouse ordered him to say his prayers and prepare for immediate death. Brown knew that there was no appeal. All Scotland was well aware by that time that soldiers were empowered to act the part of judge, jury, witness, and executioner, and had become accustomed to it. The poor man obeyed. He knelt down and prayed in such a strain that even the troopers, it is said, were impressed—at all events, their subsequent conduct would seem to countenance this belief. Their commander, however, was not much affected, for he thrice interrupted his victim, telling him that he had "given him time to pray, but not to preach."

"Sir," returned Brown, "ye know neither the nature of preaching nor praying if ye call this preaching."

"Now," said Claverhouse, "take farewell of your wife and children."

After the poor man had kissed them, Claverhouse ordered six of his men to fire; but they hesitated and finally refused. Enraged at this their commander drew a pistol, and with his own hand blew out John Brown's brains.

"What thinkest thou of thy husband now, woman?" he said, turning to the widow.

"I ever thought much good of him," she answered, "and as much now as ever."

"It were but justice to lay thee beside him," exclaimed the murderer.

"If you were permitted," she replied, "I doubt not but your cruelty would go that length."

Thus far the excitement of the dreadful scene enabled the poor creature to reply, but nature soon asserted her sway. Sinking on her knees by the side of the mangled corpse, the widow, neither observing nor caring for the departure of the dragoons, proceeded to bind up her husband's shattered skull with a kerchief, while the pent-up tears burst forth.

The house stood in a retired, solitary spot, and for some time the bereaved woman was left alone with God and her children; but before darkness closed in a human comforter was sent to her in the person of Quentin Dick.

On his arrival in Wigtown, Quentin, finding that his friends the Wilson girls had been imprisoned with an old covenanter named Mrs. McLachlan, and that he could not obtain permission to see them, resolved to pay a visit to John Brown, the carrier, who was an old friend, and who might perhaps afford him counsel regarding the Wilsons. Leaving Ramblin' Peter behind to watch every event and fetch him word if anything important should transpire, he set out and reached the desolated cottage in the evening of the day on which his friend was shot.

Quentin was naturally a reserved man, and had never been able to take a prominent part with his covenanting friends in conversation or in public prayer, but the sight of his old friend's widow in her agony, and her terrified little ones, broke down the barrier of reserve completely. Although a stern and a strong man, not prone to give way to feeling, he learned that night the full meaning of what it is to "weep with those that weep." Moreover, his tongue was unloosed, and he poured forth his soul in prayer, and quoted God's Word in a way that cheered, in no small degree, his stricken friend. During several days he remained at Priesthill, doing all in his power to assist the family, and receiving some degree of comfort in return; for strong sympathy and fellowship in sorrow had induced him to reveal the fact that he loved Margaret Wilson, who at that time lay in prison with her young sister Agnes, awaiting their trial in Wigtown.

Seated one night by the carrier's desolated hearth, where several friends had assembled to mourn with the widow, Quentin was about to commence family worship, when he was interrupted by the sudden entrance of Ramblin' Peter. The expression of his face told eloquently that he brought bad news. "The Wilsons," he said, "are condemned to be drowned with old Mrs. McLachlan."

"No' baith o' the lasses," he added, correcting

himself, "for the faither managed to git ane o' them off by a bribe o' a hundred pounds—an' that's every bodle that he owns."

"Which is to be drooned?" asked Quentin in a low voice.

"Marget—the auldest."

A deep groan burst from the shepherd as the Bible fell from his hands.

"Come!" he said to Peter, and passed quickly out of the house, without a word to those whom he left behind.

Arrived in Wigtown, the wretched man went about, wildly seeking to move the feelings of men whose hearts were like the nether millstone.

"Oh, if I only had siller!" he exclaimed to the Wilsons' father, clasping his hands in agony. "Hae ye nae mair?"

"No' anither plack," said the old man in deepest dejection. "They took all I had for Aggie."

"Ye are strang, Quentin," suggested Peter, who now understood the reason of his friend's wild despair. "Could ye no' waylay somebody an' rob them? Surely it wouldna be coonted wrang in the circumstances."

"Sin is sin, Peter. Better death than sin," returned Quentin with a grave look.

"Aweel, we maun just dee, then," said Peter in a tone of resignation.

Nothing could avert the doom of these unfortunate women. Their judges, of whom Grierson, Laird of Lagg, was one, indicted this young girl and the old woman with the ridiculous charge of rebellion, of having been at the battles of Bothwell Bridge and Airsmoss and present at twenty conventicles, as well as with refusing to swear the abjuration oath!

The innocent victims were carried to the mouth of the river Bladenoch, being guarded by troops under Major Winram, and followed by an immense crowd both of friends and spectators. Quentin Dick and his little friend Peter were among them. The former had possessed himself of a stick resembling a quarter-staff. His wild appearance and bloodshot eyes, with his great size and strength, induced people to keep out of his way. He had only just reached the spot in time. No word did he speak till he came up to Major Winram. Then he sprang forward, and said in a loud voice, "I forbid this execution in the name of God!" at the same time raising his staff.

Instantly a trooper spurred forward and cut him down from behind.

"Take him away," said Winram, and Quentin, while endeavouring to stagger to his feet, was ridden down, secured, and dragged away. Poor Peter shared his fate. So quickly and quietly was it all done that few except those quite close to them were fully aware of what had occurred. The blow on his head seemed to have stunned the shepherd, for he made no resistance while they led him a considerable distance back into the country to a retired spot, and placed him with his back against a cliff. Then the leader of the party told off six men to shoot him.

Not until they were about to present their muskets did the shepherd seem to realise his position. Then an eager look came over his face, and he said with a smile, "Ay, be quick! Maybe I'll git there first to welcome her!"

A volley followed, and the soul of Quentin Dick was released from its tenement of clay.

Peter, on seeing the catastrophe, fell backwards in a swoon, and the leader of the troop, feeling, perhaps, a touch of pity, cast him loose and left him there. Returning to the sands, the soldiers found that the martyrdom was well-nigh completed.

The mouth of the Bladenoch has been considerably modified. At this time the river's course was close along the base of the hill on which Wigtown stands. The tide had turned, and the flowing sea had already reversed the current of the river. The banks of sand were steep, and several feet high at the spot to which the martyrs were led, so that people standing on the edge were close above the inrushing stream. Two stakes had been driven into the top of the banks—one being some distance lower down the river than the other. Ropes of a few yards in length were fastened to them, and the outer ends tied round the martyrs' waists—old Mrs. McLachlan being attached to the lower post. They were then bidden prepare for death, which they did by kneeling down and engaging in fervent prayer. It is said that the younger woman repeated some passages of Scripture, and even sang part of the 25th Psalm.

At this point a married daughter of Mrs. McLachlan, named Milliken, who could not believe that the sentence would really be carried out, gave way to violent lamentations, and fainted when she saw that her mother's doom was fixed. They carried the poor creature away from the dreadful scene.

The old woman was first pushed over the brink of the river, and a soldier, thrusting her head down into the water with a halbert, held it there. This was evidently done to terrify the younger woman into submission, for, while the aged martyr was struggling in the agonies of death, one of the tormentors asked Margaret Wilson what she thought of that sight.

"What do I see?" was her reply. "I see Christ in one of His members wrestling there. Think ye that we are sufferers? No! it is Christ in us; for He sends none a warfare on his own charges."

These were her last words as she was pushed over the bank, and, like her companion, forcibly held, down with a halbert. Before she was quite suffocated, however, Winram ordered her to be dragged out, and, when able to speak, she was asked if she would pray for the King.

"I wish the salvation of all men," she replied, "and the damnation of none."

"Dear Margaret," urged a bystander in a voice of earnest entreaty, "say 'God save the King,' say 'God save the King.'"

"God save him if He will," she replied. "It is his salvation I desire."

"She has said it! she has said it!" cried the pitying bystanders eagerly.

"That won't do," cried the Laird of Lagg, coming forward at the moment, uttering a coarse oath; "let her take the test-oaths."

As this meant the repudiation of the Covenants and the submission of her conscience to the King—to her mind inexcusable sin—the martyr firmly refused to obey. She was immediately thrust back into the water, and in a few minutes more her heroic soul was with her God and Saviour.

The truth of this story—like that of John Brown of Priesthill, though attested by a letter of Claverhouse himself[1]—has been called in question, and the whole affair pronounced a myth! We have no space for controversy, but it is right to add that if it be a myth, the records of the Kirk-sessions of Kirkinner and Penninghame—which exist, and in which it is recorded—must also be mythical. The truth is, that both stories have been elaborately investigated by men of profound learning and unquestionable capacity,

---

1. See Dr. Cunningham's *History of the Church of Scotland,* vol. ii. p. 239.

and the truth of them proved "up to the hilt."

As to Graham of Claverhouse—there are people, we believe, who would whitewash the devil if he were only to present himself with a dashing person and a handsome face! But such historians as Macaulay, McCrie, McKenzie, and others, refuse to whitewash Claverhouse. Even Sir Walter Scott—who was very decidedly in sympathy with the Cavaliers—says of him in *Old Mortality*: "He was the unscrupulous agent of the Scottish Privy Council in executing the merciless severities of the Government in Scotland during the reigns of Charles the Second and James the Second;" and his latest apologist candidly admits that "it is impossible altogether to acquit Claverhouse of the charges laid to his account." We are inclined to ask, with some surprise, Why should he wish to acquit him? But Claverhouse himself, as if in prophetic cynicism, writes his own condemnation as to character thus: "In any service I have been in, I never inquired further in the laws than the orders of my superior officer." An appropriate motto for a "soldier of fortune," which might be abbreviated and paraphrased into "Stick at nothing!"

DUNNOTTAR CASTLE—Page 219

Coupling all this with the united testimony of tradition, and nearly all ancient historians, we can only wonder at the prejudice of those who would still weave a chaplet for the brow of "Bonnie Dundee."

Turning now from the south-west of Scotland, we direct attention to the eastern seaboard of Kincardine, where, perched like a sea-bird on the weatherbeaten cliffs, stands the stronghold of Dunnottar Castle.

Down in the dungeons of that rugged pile lies our friend Andrew Black, very different from the man whose fortunes we have hitherto followed. Care, torment, disease, hard usage, long confinement, and desperate anxiety have graven lines on his face that nothing but death can smooth out. Wildly-tangled hair, with a long shaggy beard and moustache, render him almost unrecognisable. Only the old unquenchable fire of his eye remains; also the kindliness of his old smile, when such a rare visitant chances once again to illuminate his worn features. Years of suffering had he undergone, and there was now little more than skin and bone of him left to undergo more.

"Let me hae a turn at the crack noo," he said, coming forward to a part of the foul miry dungeon where a crowd of male and female prisoners were endeavouring to inhale a little fresh air through a crevice in the wall. "I'm fit to choke for want o' a breath o' caller air."

As he spoke a groan from a dark corner attracted his attention. At once forgetting his own distress, he went to the place and discovered one of the prisoners, a young man, with his head pillowed on a stone, and mire some inches deep for his bed.

"Eh, Sandy, are ye sae far gane?" asked Black, kneeling beside him in tender sympathy.

"Oh, Andry, man—for a breath o' fresh air before I dee!"

"Here! ane o' ye," cried Black, "help me to carry Sandy to the crack. Wae's me, man," he added in a lower voice, "I could hae carried you ye wi' my pirlie ance, but I'm little stronger than a bairn noo."

Sandy was borne to the other side of the dungeon, and his head put close to the crevice, through which he could see the white ripples on the summer sea far below.

A deep inspiration seemed for a moment to give new life—then a prolonged sigh, and the freed happy soul swept from the dungeons of earth to the realms of celestial, light and liberty.

"He's breathin' the air o' Paradise noo," said Black, as he assisted to remove the dead man from the opening which the living were so eager to reach.

"Ye was up in the ither dungeon last night," he said, turning to the man who had aided him; "what was a' the groans an' cries aboot?"

"Torturin' the puir lads that tried to escape," answered the man with a dark frown.

"Hm! I thoucht as muckle. They were gey hard on them, I dar'say?"

"They were that! Ye see, the disease that's broke oot amang them—whatever it is—made some o' them sae desprit that they got through the wundy that looks to the sea an' creepit alang the precipice. It was a daft-like thing to try in the daylight; but certain death would hae been their lot, I suspec', if they had ventured on a precipice like that i' the dark. Some women washin' doon below saw them and gied the alarm. The gairds cam', the hue and cry was raised, the yetts were shut and fifteen were catched an' brought back—but twenty-five got away. My heart is wae for the fifteen. They were laid on their backs on benches; their hands were bound doon to the foot o' the forms, an' burnin' matches were putt atween every finger, an' the sodgers blew on them to keep them alight. The governor, ye see, had ordered this to gang on withoot stoppin' for three oors! Some o' the puir fallows were deid afore the end o' that time, an' I'm thinkin' the survivors'll be crippled for life."

While listening to the horrible tale Andrew Black resolved on an attempt to escape that very night.

"Wull ye gang wi' me?" he asked of the only comrade whom he thought capable of making the venture; but the comrade shook his head. "Na," he said, "I'll no' try. They've starved me to that extent that I've nae strength left. I grow dizzy at the vera thoucht. But d'ye think the wundy's big enough to let ye through?"

"Oo ay," returned Black with a faint smile. "I was ower stoot for't ance, but it's an ill wund that blaws nae guid. Stervation has made me thin enough noo."

That night, when all—even the harassed prisoners—in Dunnottar Castle were asleep, except the sentinels, the desperate man forced himself with difficulty through the very small window of the dungeon. It was unbarred, because, opening out on the face of an almost sheer precipice, it was thought that nothing without wings could escape from it. Black, however, had been accustomed to precipices from boyhood. He had observed a narrow ledge just under the window, and hoped that it might lead to something. Just below it he could see another and narrower ledge. What was beyond that he knew not—and did not much care!

Once outside, with his breast pressed against the wall of rock, he passed along pretty quickly, considering that he could not see more than a few yards before him. But presently he came to the end of the ledge, and by no stretching out of foot or hand could he find another projection of any kind. He had now to face the great danger of sliding down to the lower ledge, and his heart beat audibly against his ribs as he gazed into the profound darkness below. Indecision was no part of Andrew Black's character. Breathing a silent prayer for help and deliverance, he sat down on the ledge with his feet overhanging the abyss. For one moment he reconsidered his position. Behind him were torture, starvation, prolonged misery, and almost certain death. Below was perhaps instantaneous death, or possible escape.

He pushed off, again commending his soul to God, and slid down. For an instant destruction seemed inevitable, but next moment his heels struck the lower ledge and he remained fast. With an earnest "Thank God!" he began to creep along. The ledge conducted him to safer ground, and in another quarter of an hour he was free!

To get as far and as quickly as possible from Dunnottar was now his chief aim. He travelled at his utmost speed till daybreak, when he crept into a dry ditch, and, overcome by fatigue, forgot his sorrow in profound unbroken slumber. Rising late in the afternoon, he made his way to a cottage and begged for bread. They must have suspected what he was and where he came from, but they were friendly, for they gave him a loaf and a few pence without asking questions.

Thus he travelled by night and slept by day till he made his way to Edinburgh, which he entered one evening in the midst of a crowd of people, and went straight to Candlemaker Row.

Mrs. Black, Mrs. Wallace, Jean Black, and poor Agnes Wilson were in the old room when a tap was heard at the door, which immediately opened, and a gaunt, dishevelled, way-worn man appeared. Mrs. Black was startled at first, for the man, regardless of the other females, advanced towards her. Then sudden light seemed to flash in her eyes as she extended both hands.

"Mither!" was all that Andrew could say as he grasped them, fell on his knees, and, with a profound sigh, laid his head upon her lap.

# Chapter XII

Many months passed away, during which Andrew Black, clean-shaved, brushed-up, and converted into a very respectable, ordinary-looking artisan, carried on the trade of a turner, in an underground cellar in one of the most populous parts of the Cowgate. Lost in the crowd was his idea of security. And he was not far wrong. His cellar had a way of escape through a back door. Its grated window, under the level of the street, admitted light to his whirling lathe, but, aided by dirt on the glass, it baffled the gaze of the curious.

His evenings were spent in Candlemaker Row, where, seated by the window with his mother, Mrs.

Wallace, and the two girls, he smoked his pipe and commented on Scotland's woes while gazing across the tombs at the glow in the western sky. Ramblin' Peter—no longer a beardless boy, but a fairly well-grown and good-looking youth—was a constant visitor at the Row. Aggie Wilson had taught him the use of his tongue, but Peter was not the man to use it in idle flirtation—nor Aggie the girl to listen if he had done so. They had both seen too much of the stern side of life to condescend on trifling.

Once, by a superhuman effort, and with an alarming flush of the countenance, Peter succeeded in stammering a declaration of his sentiments. Aggie, with flaming cheeks and downcast eyes, accepted the declaration, and the matter was settled; that was all, for the subject had rushed upon both of them, as it were, unexpectedly, and as they were in the public street at the time and the hour was noon, further demonstration might have been awkward.

Thereafter they were understood to be "keeping company." But they were a grave couple. If an eavesdropper had ventured to listen, sober talk alone would have repaid the sneaking act, and, not unfrequently, reference would have been heard in tones of deepest pathos to dreadful scenes that had occurred on the shores of the Solway, or sorrowful comments on the awful fate of beloved friends who had been banished to "the plantations."

One day Jean—fair-haired, blue-eyed, pensive Jean—was seated in the cellar with her uncle. She had brought him his daily dinner in a tin can, and he having just finished it, was about to resume his work while the niece rose to depart. Time had transformed Jean from a pretty girl into a beautiful woman, but there was an expression of profound melancholy on her once bright face which never left it now, save when a passing jest called up for an instant a feeble reminiscence of the sweet old smile.

"Noo, Jean, awa' wi' ye. I'll never get thae parritch-sticks feenished if ye sit haverin' there."

Something very like the old smile lighted up Jean's face as she rose, and with a "weel, good-day, uncle," left the cellar to its busy occupant.

Black was still at work, and the shadows of evening were beginning to throw the inner end of the cellar into gloom, when the door slowly opened and a man entered stealthily. The unusual action, as well as the appearance of the man, caused Black to seize hold of a heavy piece of wood that leaned against his lathe. The thought of being discovered and sent back to Dunnottar, or hanged, had implanted in our friend a salutary amount of caution, though it had not in the slightest degree affected his nerve or his cool promptitude in danger. He had deliberately made up his mind to remain quiet as long as he should be let alone, but if discovered, to escape or die in the attempt.

The intruder was a man of great size and strength, but as he seemed to be alone, Black quietly leaned the piece of wood against the lathe again in a handy position.

"Ye seem to hae been takin' lessons frae the cats lately, to judge from yer step," said Black. "Shut the door, man, behint ye. There's a draft i' this place that'll be like to gie ye the rheumatiz."

The man obeyed, and, advancing silently, stood before the lathe. There was light enough to reveal the fact that his countenance was handsome, though bronzed almost to the colour of mahogany, while the lower part of it was hidden by a thick beard and a heavy moustache.

Black, who began to see that the strange visitor had nothing of the appearance of one sent to arrest him, said, in a half-humorous, remonstrative tone—

"Maybe ye're a furriner, an' dinna understan' mainners, but it's as weel to tell ye that I expec' men to tak' aff their bannets when they come into *my* hoose."

Without speaking the visitor removed his cap. Black recognised him in an instant.

"Wull Wallace!" he gasped in a hoarse whisper, as he sprang forward and laid violent hands on his old friend. "Losh, man! are my een leein'? is't possable? Can this be *you?*"

"Yes, thank God, it is indeed—"

He stopped short, for Andrew, albeit unaccustomed, like most of his countrymen, to give way to ebullitions of strong feeling, threw his long arms around his friend and fairly hugged him. He did not, indeed, condescend on a Frenchman's kiss, but he gave him a stage embrace and a squeeze that was worthy of a bear.

"Your force is not much abated, I see—or rather, feel," said Will Wallace, when he was released.

"Abated!" echoed Black, "it's little need, in thae awfu' times. But, man, *your* force has increased, if I'm no mista'en."

"Doubtless—it is natural, after having toiled with the slaves in Barbadoes for so many years. The work was kill or cure out there. But tell me—my mother—and yours?"

"Oh, they're baith weel and hearty, thank the Lord," answered Black. "But what for d'ye no speer after Jean?" he added in a somewhat disappointed tone.

"Because I don't need to. I've seen her already, and know that she is well."

"Seen her!" exclaimed Andrew in surprise.

"Ay, you and Jean were seated alone at the little window in the Candlemaker Raw last night about ten o'clock, and I was standing by a tombstone in the Greyfriars Churchyard admiring you. I did not like to present myself just then, for fear of alarming the dear girl too much, and then I did not dare to come here to-day till the gloamin'. I only arrived yesterday."

"Weel, weel! The like o' this bates a'. Losh man! I hope it's no a dream. Nip me, man, to mak sure. Sit doon, sit doon, an' let's hear a' aboot it."

The story was a long one. Before it was quite

finished the door was gently opened, and Jean Black herself entered. She had come, as was her wont every night, to walk home with her uncle.

Black sprang up.

"Jean, my wummin," he said, hastily putting on his blue bonnet, "there's no light eneuch for ye to be intryduced to my freend here, but ye can hear him if ye canna see him. I'm gaun oot to see what sort o' a night it is. He'll tak' care o' ye till I come back."

Without awaiting a reply he went out and shut the door, and the girl turned in some surprise towards the stranger.

"Jean!" he said in a low voice, holding out both hands.

Jean did not scream or faint. Her position in life, as well as her rough experiences, forbade such weakness, but it did not forbid—well, it is not our province to betray confidences! All we can say is, that when Andrew Black returned to the cellar, after a prolonged and no doubt scientific inspection of the weather, he found that the results of the interview had been quite satisfactory—eminently so!

Need we say that there were rejoicing and thankful hearts in Candlemaker Row that night? We think not. If any of the wraiths of the Covenanters were hanging about the old churchyard, and had peeped in at the well-known back window about the small hours of the morning, they would have seen our hero, clasping his mother with his right arm and Jean with his left. He was encircled by an eager group—composed of Mrs. Black and Andrew, Jock Bruce, Ramblin' Peter, and Aggie Wilson—who listened to the stirring tale of his adventures, or detailed to him the not less stirring and terrible history of the long period that had elapsed since he was torn from them, as they had believed, for ever.

Next morning Jean accompanied her lover to the workshop of her uncle, who had preceded them, as he usually went to work about daybreak.

"Are ye no feared," asked Jean, with an anxious look in her companion's face, "that some of your auld enemies may recognise you? You're so big and—and—" (she thought of the word handsome, but substituted) "odd-looking."

"There is little fear, Jean. I've been so long away that most of the people—the enemies at least—who knew me must have left; besides, my bronzed face and bushy beard form a sufficient disguise, I should think."

"I'm no sure o' that," returned the girl, shaking

her head doubtfully; "an' it seems to me that the best thing ye can do will be to gang to the workshop every mornin' before it's daylight. Have ye fairly settled to tak' to Uncle Andrew's trade?"

"Yes. Last night he and I arranged it while you were asleep. I must work, you know, to earn my living, and there is no situation so likely to afford such effectual concealment. Bruce offered to take me on again, but the smiddy is too public, and too much frequented by soldiers. Ah, Jean! I fear that our wedding-day is a long way off yet, for, although I could easily make enough to support you in comfort if there were no difficulties to hamper me, there is not much chance of my making a fortune, as Andrew Black says, by turning parritch-sticks and peeries!"

Wallace tried to speak lightly, but could not disguise a tone of despondency.

"Your new King," he continued, "seems as bad as the old one, if not worse. From all I hear he seems to have set his heart on bringing the country back again to Popery, and black will be the look-out if he succeeds in doing that. He has quarrelled, they say, with his bishops, and in his anger is carrying matters against them with a high hand. I fear that there is woe in store for poor Scotland yet."

"It may be so," returned Jean sadly. "The Lord knows what is best; but He can make the wrath of man to praise Him. Perhaps," she added, looking up with a solemn expression on her sweet face, "perhaps, like Quentin Dick an' Margaret Wilson, you an' I may never wed."

They had reached the east end of the Grassmarket as she spoke, and had turned into it before she observed that they were going wrong, but Wallace explained that he had been directed by Black to call on Ramblin' Peter, who lived there, and procure from him some turning-tools. On the way they were so engrossed with each other that they did not at first observe the people hurrying towards the lower end of the market. Then they became aware that an execution was about to take place.

"The old story," muttered Wallace, while an almost savage scowl settled on his face.

"Let us hurry by," said Jean in a low tone. At the moment the unhappy man who was about to be executed raised his voice to speak, as was the custom in those times.

Jean started, paused, and turned deadly pale.

"I ken the voice," she exclaimed.

As the tones rose in strength she turned towards the gallows and almost dragged her companion after her in her eagerness to get near.

"It's Mr. Renwick," she said, "the dear servant o' the Lord!"

Wallace, on seeing her anxiety, elbowed his way through the crowd somewhat forcibly, and thus made way for Jean till they stood close under the gallows. It was a woeful sight in one sense, for it was the murder of a fair and goodly as well as godly man in the prime of life; yet it was a grand sight, inasmuch as it was a noble witnessing unto death for God and truth and justice in the face of prejudice, passion, and high-handed tyranny.

The martyr had been trying to address the crowd for some time, but had been barbarously interrupted by the beating of drums. Just then a curate approached him and said, "Mr. Renwick, own our King, and we will pray for you."

"It's that scoundrel, the Reverend George Lawless," murmured Wallace in a deep and bitter tone.

"I am come here," replied the martyr, "to bear my

testimony against you, and all such as you are."

"Own our King, and pray for him, whatever ye say of us," returned the curate.

"I will discourse no more with you," rejoined Renwick. "I am in a little to appear before Him who is King of kings and Lord of lords, who shall pour shame, contempt, and confusion on all the kings of the earth who have not ruled for Him."

After this Renwick—as was usual with the martyrs when about to finish their course—sang, read a portion of Scripture, and prayed, in the midst of considerable interruption from the drums. He also managed to address the spectators. Among the sentences that reached the ears of Jean and Wallace were the following:—

"I am come here this day to lay down my life for adhering to the truths of Christ... I die as a Presbyterian Protestant... I own the Word of God as the rule of faith and manners... I leave my testimony against... all encroachments made on Christ's rights, who is the Prince of the kings of the earth."

The noise of the drums rendered his voice inaudible at this point, and the executioner, advancing, tied a napkin over his eyes. He was then ordered to go up the ladder. To a friend who stood by him he gave his last messages. Among them were the words—

"Keep your ground, and the Lord will provide you teachers and ministers; and when He comes He will make these despised truths glorious in the earth."

His last words were— "Lord, into thy hands I commit my spirit; for thou hast redeemed me, Lord God of truth."

Thus fell the last, as it turned out, of the martyrs of the Covenants, on the 17th of February 1688. But it did not seem to Will Wallace that the storm of twenty-eight long years had almost blown over, as he glanced at the scowling brows and compressed lips of the upturned faces around him.

"Come—come away, Jean," he said quickly, as he felt the poor girl hang heavily on his arm, and observed the pallor of her face.

"Ay, let's gang hame," she said faintly.

As Will turned to go he encountered a face that was very familiar. The owner of it gazed at him inquiringly. It was that of his old comrade in arms, Glendinning. Stooping over his companion as if to address her, Wallace tried to conceal his face and pushed quickly through the crowd. Whether Glendinning had recognised him or not, he could not be sure, but from that day forward he became much more careful in his movements, went regularly to his work with Andrew Black before daylight, and did not venture to return each night till after dark. It was a weary and irksome state of things, but better— as Black sagaciously remarked—than being imprisoned on the Bass Rock or shut up in Dunnottar Castle. But the near presence of Jean Black had, no doubt, more to do with the resignation of our hero to his position than the fear of imprisonment.

As time passed, things in the political horizon looked blacker than ever. The King began to show himself more and more in his true colours—as one who had thoroughly made up his mind to rule as an absolute monarch and to reclaim the kingdom to Popery. Among other things he brought troops over from Ireland to enforce his will, some of his English troops having made it abundantly plain that they could not be counted on to obey the mandates of one who wished to arrogate to himself unlimited power, and showed an utter disregard of the rights of the people. Indeed, on all hands the King's friends began to forsake him, and even his own children fell away from him at last.

Rumours of these things, more or less vague, had been reaching Edinburgh from time to time, causing uneasiness in the minds of some and hope in the hearts of others.

One night the usual party of friends had assembled to sup in the dwelling of Mrs. Black. It was the Sabbath. Wallace and Black had remained close all day—with the exception of an hour before daylight in the morning when they had gone out for exercise. It was one of those dreary days not unknown to Auld Reekie, which are inaugurated with a persistent drizzle, continued with a "Scotch mist," and dismissed with an even down-pour. Yet it was by no means a dismal day to our friends of Candlemaker Row. They were all more or less earnestly religious as well as intellectual, so that intercourse in reference to the things of the Kingdom of God, and reading the Word, with a free-and-easy commentary by Mrs. Black and much acquiescence on the part of Mrs. Wallace, and occasional disputations between Andrew and Bruce, kept them lively and well employed until supper-time.

The meal had just been concluded when heavy footfalls were heard on the stair outside, and in another moment there was a violent knocking at the door. The men sprang up, and instinctively grasped the weapons that came first to hand. Wallace seized the poker—a new and heavy one—Andrew the shovel, and Jock Bruce the tongs, while Ramblin' Peter possessed himself of a stout rolling-pin. Placing themselves hastily in front of the women, who had drawn together and retreated to a corner, they stood on the defensive while Mrs. Black demanded to know who knocked so furiously "on a Sabbath nicht."

Instead of answering, the visitors burst the door open, and half-a-dozen of the town-guard sprang in and levelled their pikes.

"Yield yourselves!" cried their leader. "I arrest you in the King's name!"

But the four men showed no disposition to yield, and the resolute expression of their faces induced their opponents to hesitate.

"I ken o' nae King in this realm," said Andrew Black in a deep stern voice, "an' we refuse to set oor necks under the heel o' a usurpin' tyrant."

"Do your duty, men," said a man who had kept in the background, but who now stepped to the front.

"Ha! this is your doing, Glendinning," exclaimed Wallace, who recognised his old comrade. The sergeant had obviously been promoted, for he wore the costume of a commissioned officer.

"Ay, I have an auld score to settle wi' you, Wallace, an' I hope to see you an' your comrades swing in the Grassmarket before lang."

"Ye'll niver see that, my man," said Black, as he firmly grasped the shovel. "Ye ha'ena gotten us yet, an' it's my opeenion that you an' your freends'll be in kingdom-come before we swing, if ye try to tak' us alive. Oot o' this hoose, ye scoondrels!"

So saying, Black made a spring worthy of a royal Bengal tiger, turned aside the pike of the foremost man, and brought the shovel down on his iron headpiece with such force that he was driven back into the passage or landing, and fell prostrate. Black was so ably and promptly seconded by his stalwart comrades that the room was instantly cleared. Glendinning, driven back by an irresistible blow from the rolling-pin, tripped over the fallen man and went headlong down the winding stairs, at the bottom of which he lay dead, with his neck broken by the fall.

But the repulse thus valiantly effected did not avail them much, for the leader of the guard had reinforcements below, which he now called up. Before the door could be shut these swarmed into the room and drove the defenders back into their corner. The leader hesitated, however, to give the order to advance on them, partly, it may be, because he wished to induce submission and thus avoid bloodshed, and partly, no doubt, because of the terrible aspect of the four desperate men, who, knowing that the result of their capture would be almost certain death, preceded by imprisonment, and probably torture, had evidently made up their minds to fight to the death.

At that critical moment a quick step was heard upon the stair, and the next moment the Reverend Frank Selby entered the room.

"Just in time, I see," he said in a cool nonchalant manner that was habitual to him. "I think, sir," he added, turning to the leader of the guard, "that it may be as well to draw off your men and return to the guard-room."

"I'll do that," retorted the man sharply, "when I receive orders from my superiors. Just now I'll do my duty."

"Of course you will do what is right, my good sir," replied the Reverend Frank; "yet I venture to think you will regret neglecting my advice, which, allow me to assure you, is given in quite a friendly and disinterested spirit. I have just left the precincts of the Council Chamber, where I was told by a friend in office that the Councillors have been thrown into a wild and excusable state of alarm by the news that William, Prince of Orange, who, perhaps you may know, is James's son-in-law and nephew, has landed in Torbay with 15,000 Dutchmen. He comes by invitation of the nobles and clergy of the kingdom to take possession of the Crown which our friend James has forfeited, and James himself has fled to France—one of the few wise things of which he has ever been guilty. It is further reported that the panic-stricken Privy Council here talks of throwing open all the prison-doors in Edinburgh, after which it will voluntarily dissolve itself. If it could do so in prussic acid or some chemical solvent suited to the purpose, its exit would be hailed as all the more appropriate. Meanwhile, I am of opinion that all servants of the Council would do well to retire into as much privacy as possible, and then maintain a careful look-out for squalls."

Having delivered this oration to the gaping guard, the Reverend Frank crossed the room and went through the forbidden and dangerous performance of shaking hands heartily with the "rebels."

He was still engaged in this treasonable act, and the men of the town-guard had not yet recovered from their surprise, when hurrying footsteps were again heard on the stair, and a man of the town-guard sprang into the room, went to his chief, and whispered in his ear. The result was, that, with a countenance expressing mingled surprise and anxiety, the officer led his men from the scene, and left the long-persecuted Covenanters in peace.

"Losh, man! div 'ee railly think the news can be true?" asked Andrew Black, after they had settled down and heard it all repeated.

"Indeed I do," said the Reverend Frank earnestly, "and I thank God that a glorious Revolution seems to have taken place, and hope that the long, long years of persecution are at last drawing to a close."

And Frank Selby was right. The great Revolution of 1688, which set William and Mary on the throne, also banished the tyrannical and despotic house of Stuart for ever; opened the prison gates to the Covenanters; restored to some extent the reign of justice and mercy; crushed, if it did not kill, the heads of Popery and absolute power, and sent a great wave of praise and thanksgiving over the whole land. Prelacy was no longer forced upon Scotland. The rights and liberties of the people were secured, and the day had at last come which crowned the struggles and sufferings of half a century. As Mrs. Black remarked—

"Surely the blood o' the martyrs has not been shed in vain!"

.    .    .    .    .    .

But what of the fortunes of those whose adventures we have followed so long? Whatever they were, the record has not been written, yet we have been told by a man whose name we may not divulge, but who is an unquestionable authority on the subject, that soon after the persecution about which we have been writing had ceased, a farmer of the name of Black settled down among the "bonnie hills of Galloway," not far from the site of the famous Communion stones on Skeoch Hill, where he took to himself a wife; that another farmer, a married man named Wallace, went and built a cottage and settled there on a farm close beside Black; that a certain R Peter became shepherd to the farmer Black, and, with his wife, served him faithfully all the days of his life; that the families of these men were very large, the men among them being handsome and stalwart, the women modest and beautiful, and that all of them were loyal subjects and earnest, enthusiastic Covenanters. It has been also said, though we do not vouch for the accuracy of the statement, that in the Kirk-session books of the neighbouring kirk of Irongray there may be found among the baptisms such names as Andrew Wallace and Will Black, Quentin Dick Black, and Jock Bruce Wallace; also an Aggie, a Marion, and an Isabel Peter, besides several Jeans scattered among the three families.

It has likewise been reported, on reliable authority, that the original Mr. Black, whose Christian name was Andrew, was a famous teller of stories and narrator of facts regarding the persecution of the Covenanters, especially of the awful killing-time, when the powers of darkness were let loose on the land to do their worst, and when the blood of Scotland's martyrs flowed like water.

Between 1661, when the Marquis of Argyll was beheaded, and 1668, when James Renwick suffered, there were murdered for the cause of Christ and Christian liberty about 18,000 noble men and women, some of whom were titled, but the most of whom were unknown to earthly fame. It is a marvellous record of the power of God; and well may we give all honour to the martyr band while we exclaim with the "Ayrshire Elder":—

> "O for the brave true hearts of old,
>    That bled when the banner perished!
> O for the faith that was strong in death—
>    The faith that our fathers cherished.
>
> "The banner might fall, but the spirit lived,
>    And liveth for evermore;
> And Scotland claims as her noblest names
>    The Covenant men of yore."

**THE END**